by TOM J SANDY

SCATE

by TOM J SANDY

Published by Eye 5

ISBN 0-9546897-3-9

Published 2004 by Eye 5.
Text © Tom J Sandy. For reproduction permission, please contact Eye 5.

Eye 5
15 Spruce Avenue
Great Dunmow
Essex
CM6 1YY
United Kingdom

www.eye5.org.uk

*For Audrey, and sensible motorists
and cyclists everywhere*

CONTENTS

EYE 5

PROLOGUE

The Doctor Leaves His Card

THE police constable stepped back and examined his hands. They were red and had some sticky substance on them.

"Jeeze, it's tough," gasped PC Richard Harolds.

"Here, let me have a go," said his colleague, PC Frank Davies.

PC Davies gripped the plastic plate with his rough hands. He grunted several times. The grunts and his considerable strength could not detach the plate from the front of the speed camera.

"Call the maintenance boys. Not our bloody problem," suggested PC Harolds, still struggling to scrape the sticky stuff from his hands.

PC Davies stepped back, annoyed at his failure. He checked his hands, too, and said: "Yeah. Too tough for me to crack it. What is that stuff anyway?"

When the maintenance boy arrived a good half hour later they discovered the source of their frustration.

"Ah! Our pal again," said cheery Joe as he started chipping away at the plate with a small chisel.

"Who's our pal?" asked PC Harolds.

"Dr Glue," replied Fred even more cheerily.

"Dr Glue?"

"Yep. Wonderful sense of humour he has, too. This is my fourth today."

"Fourth! The Super'll be going spare!" gasped PC Davies.

"He is," chuckled Joe Franklyn, a 28-year-old with nine years behind him as all-round dogsbody with the Lancashire Constabulary. "This one could send him over the edge."

'This one' was one of the local police force's most-prized Gatsos - earning anything up to £6,000 an hour. Situated on the M6 by Preston, it caught speeding motorists and flashed images digitally to the traffic headquarters. Each offender was obliged to cough up £60.

It was two o'clock on a surprisingly pleasant February afternoon and Joe explained to the two police officers that he had been on the go since 8am. Two others calls on the M6 and one on the route to the coast. Merseyside police had dealt with two calls, too.

"The good doctor had a busy night," added Joe. "I smashed the first couple off with my hammer but the Super wants them nice and neat now so the boys can check for prints. Fat chance of that, if you ask me."

Joe had finally prised the plate free, gently as he could so as to keep Superintendent Charleston happy. He placed it in a plastic wallet.

The three men stared at the Gatso; its lens was shattered and wires had been clipped. There was that sticky substance coating it. There was a businesscard placed at an angle in the substance.

PC Harolds took it and read:

Dr Glue: Roadside assistance a speciality

"Yep, a real funny guy," said Joe. "Now, I'm no detective but if you want my advice, don't go looking for a medical man. The guy you're looking for has a boot full of superglue. Strong stuff it is. Stronger than any I have come across before."

"But why put the plate over a smashed camera?" asked PC Davies.

"It's his signature, I suppose," replied Joe. "Plus, look at the amount of police time he's wasted already today. The third one I did was strange 'cos the camera wasn't smashed. It felt like he was keeping us on our toes.

"Anyway, how come this beauty wasn't reported earlier? Makes a mint, doesn't it?"

"It was reported earlier," said PC Harolds. "We got the call first thing this morning. Unfortunately for the Super's coffers we got called away on PROPER police work."

TWO DAYS LATER

The forensic department's report revealed no prints on the underside of the two salvaged plastic plates. The outsides matched the prints of four, red-faced serving police officers.

Superintendent Charleston was incandescent.

"I want Dr Bloody Glue....now!" he bawled.

CHAPTER ONE

Gavin Grovels In The Dock

TWELVE MONTHS EARLIER

GAVIN LLOYD didn't have a leg to stand on.
FLASH!
FLASH!
FLASH!
FLASH!

Four of the buggers had nailed him. Four in just six months. Unlucky or just plain stupid; he couldn't make up his mind as he prepared to enter the dock and plead. To plead for what? He wasn't even sure of that.

To plead for mercy, forgiveness, understanding?

He tried all three during his five minutes of infamy in the dock.

He had heeded the advice of Lisa, the police officer who drank from time to time at his local pub, and taken public transport to Harlow Magistrates' court. That was an ordeal in itself; a test run which met all his fears.

The north-west Essex village of Great Wilton was poorly served. The railway station had closed in the 1960s cutbacks and buses ran infrequently, though regular users informed him that the expansion of the airport had brought about a vast improvement.

Small mercies, Gavin thought, as he embarked on the 90-minute journey that would have taken a third of that by car.

Waiting in line was not something Gavin did well. But he waited for the bus that took him to the railway station 12 miles away. Then he strolled up and down the platform as he waited for the train to take him to Harlow. At Harlow his patience ran out and he grabbed a taxi to the court.

The court was having lunch and was pleasantly peaceful. Gavin had expected to encounter the dregs of society, but just a few smartly-dressed types hung around the entrance hall.

They had one thing in common: all were fidgeting and seemed ill at ease. Gavin realised he was fidgeting, too. His hands weren't sure what to do, his eyes unsure where to look. Yes, Gavin himself was ill at ease among a growing throng of fellow fidgeters.

Still, at least there were no hardened criminals glaring at him threateningly.

He tried not to stare at the people around him: the couple talking earnestly on the bench by the far wall; the flustered pin-striped 50-some who kept checking his watch; the spotty youngster who had paid two visits to the gents in the ten minutes Gavin had been there. He's 19 at most, thought Gavin, and clearly unaccustomed to wearing a tie.

A door creaked open and a uniformed man walked purposefully towards a central desk. He spread out a sheaf of papers in front of him and began making marks on them. Gavin didn't suspect they were exam papers.

"The court will commence in ten minutes," he announced, barely looking up from his papers.

A few seconds of absolute silence followed until he walked to a large notice board and pinned up several sheets of paper.

Then, head up this time, he made another announcement: "Courts A and B are sitting today. Check which court you are expected in here." He pointed at the notice board. "If you have any questions, ask myself or one of my colleagues. This is a non-smoking building."

A small group of people puffed away outside oblivious to his announcements.

Strangely, Gavin hadn't felt like joining them.

He checked the notices. It matched his letter, and he was due in Court B at 2.15pm to answer charges and explain his fourth speeding offence in six months.

He glanced at all the names, closely typed on six sheets of A4 paper. There must have been a couple of hundred names. All appeared to be charged with some kind of motoring offence. That explained the absence of the gangsters Gavin had expected to encounter that day: Tuesday was the day the court caught up with society's bad, careless, drunk, fast, negligent drivers. And the plain stupid ones.

Gavin ran through his defence in his head. He hadn't sought legal representation outside the free advice from friendly WPC Lisa at the Dog And Duck back home.

"A brief is unlikely to get you off," she had told him. "Not for something like this. But I would advise you to put in a personal appearance. They'd view a postal plea as an insult to the court. You never know, you may strike lucky."

Until then, Gavin had considered pleading guilty by post, not seeing much point in having to look at smug faces sentencing him.

His mental pleas were interrupted as he heard three names read out. His was the last. He hadn't noticed more uniforms enter the reception hall.

He and the other two awaiting trial approached the usher who had called them. All three were to go into the courtroom and would be dealt with in due course.

Gavin had to sit through two cases before his turn. It was enlightening. Both accused men had solicitors to plead for them. Had Gavin made an almighty mistake?

Neither man spoke except to confirm their basic details.

The first case involved a man maybe a couple of years younger than Gavin's 35 years.

Gavin's ears pricked up when he realised the man was charged with speeding and had been caught on film by one of the new Gatsos on the M11. Gavin knew it well. He did by now, anyway.

The solicitor seemed hilarious in his deference to the magistrates' bench. A stern-faced woman in her fifties and a poker-faced old-soldier type sat either side of the Chief Magistrate. The Chief Magistrate looked a reasonable guy, thought Gavin. Clearly a self-made businessman, plain-speaking and seemingly efficient.

All three listened with varying degrees of apparent interest as the solicitor explained how his client had come to be driving at 95 miles per hour in a 50 zone.

His client, you see, had borrowed his boss's new 7 Series BMW and didn't quite realise the supreme power of the beast. His own Cavalier was being serviced, you see.

Plus the 50 zone had only just been introduced while road maintenance was carried out, you see.

The lawyer droned on about how his client had an exemplary driving history, was a key, loyal employee. And, you see, the client needed his licence to keep his job.

The magistrates saw clearly enough. A quick huddle and the verdict was solemnly announced: 200 quid fine, six points on his licence. No ban, Mr Lucky shook his solicitor's hand and left court smiling.

Case number two saw an old guy's solicitor tell the bench how his client happened to have knocked a motorcyclist and his pillion passsenger off their bike on the blessed M11.

His client had been driving a party of old folk back from an outing on the East Anglia coast. It was dark and raining; the road was slippery and the driver must have misjudged the distance of the lights approaching his coach. He had been driving for 50 years, had a clean licence and this part-time coach-driving job had helped him recover from the loss of his wife two years previously.

At least the solicitor didn't feel the need to ask the bench if they saw what he was on about.

Another lucky man left the court owing them 150 quid and was saddled with a 275 bill for bike repairs. Thankfully, neither victim had been physically injured, stressed the Chief Magistrate as he warned the accused about the very high standards expected from public service vehicles.

The man nodded humbly and thanked the court.

"Gavin Lloyd," proclaimed the clerk to the court in a clipped voice.

Gavin shot up. He knew it was his turn but the sound of his name still made him jump.

He approached the bench and managed to croak a feeble "Yes" as the clerk checked his personal details.

The clerk informed the bench that this was Mr Lloyd's fourth speeding offence and that the customary three-point penalty would take him to 12 points under the totting up procedure.

TWELVE POINTS. Dreaded by all motorists, bringing with it an automatic disqualification from driving the roads of Great Britain.

The Chief Magistrate asked Gavin if there was anything he wished to tell the court.

Gavin's "Yes, please" was slightly less feeble than before but still unlikely to strike fear into a parade ground squaddie. He was instructed to enter the dock and swear on the Bible that he would tell the truth or be condemned to a fate worse than a driving ban.

He told the truth. That was his way, even if it did sound ridiculous to Gavin that a reasonably-intelligent guy like him could be caught hook, line and sinker on camera four times in such a short space of time.

Yes, he readily confessed that he had broken the respective speed limits - three times on the M11 and once on the A120. But the court already knew this as he had paid the statutory £60 fine and had the three points put on his driving licence for each of his first three offences.

This fourth one was the problem. So here goes, he mentally crossed his fingers...

"Well, first I would like to apologise to the court for breaking the speed limits," still not quite Regimental Sergeant Major-quality but less croaky.

"But I would like you to take into consideration that all my offences were captured on speed cameras outside rush-hour. Traffic was certainly very light on three occasions when I was returning home from work in the early hours of the morning."

Gavin looked up, the bench appeared to be taking interest. He fought the urge to launch into a tirade against Gatsos.

"And I would like the court to please take into account my circumstances in assessing punishment."

That came out exactly as Gavin had rehearsed before his mirror over the past few days.

"I live in Great Wilton and work irregular shifts in London."

This was grovel-time and Gavin felt uncomfortable but pressed on. Maybe he should have enlisted a solicitor.

"It would be very difficult for me to commute to work via public transport."

He had thought of saying "impossible to commute" but stuck to the "very difficult" truth.

"Great Wilton has no train service and buses are very limited outside the normal business hours."

That was it, no grand finale delivered with a Wildean flourish; just an abrupt ending to a please-be-gentle-with-me plea.

The Chief Magistrate looked at Gavin and surprised him by softly saying "Thank you."

He studied some papers on his bench before asking Gavin: "Is there anyone who relies on you and your car?"

"Well, as I have said, it really is essential for me to get to work...and the kids treat me as their personal taxi service."

The last words came out half-jokingly, but no-one was laughing, least of all Gavin.

"Yes, but what I mean is: Do you have any old or infirm relative who relies on you to drive them around? To hospital, for example. Or do you provide driving for any charity? Your work problems and your children's social lives are not the concern of this court."

Gavin thought hard for a moment, a fictitious doddery old aunt flashed through his mind. He was at a loss as what to say.

"No, sir," the feeble croak had returned. The Chief Magistrate had given him an escape route and Gavin had been unable to find it.

A quick conference between the three dispensers of justice then the Chief Magistrate addressed Gavin:

"We are fining you £250 for the speeding offence. This takes you above the 12-point mark and so you are disqualified from driving for six months. The disqualification period commences immediately so do not attempt to drive away from this court. You will also be required to pay £70 court costs."

Gavin was led away by an usher who sat him down and discussed payment of the fine and costs. Gavin was still in shock as he scribbled out a cheque. SIX MONTHS!

Ouch! Ouch! Ouch! Ouch! Ouch! Bloody Ouch!

He had been expecting three. Six months! He was certain a workmate had been handed three months. He was also sure WPC Lisa had told him to expect that. At least Lisa had advised him correctly against driving to court.

He left the court to the sound of a woman's voice berating the Gatsos on the M11. He didn't look back to check the countenances on the bench.

He was shocked and angry. Both emotions fought for supremacy.

Gavin had mentally prepared himself for a three-month ban. He had arranged to take a week's leave each month, though February-April was hardly his preferred choice of vacation time. That would have left him nine working weeks to worry about.

He had mapped out routes through the tangled mess which passed for public transport.

He worked the late shifts, manning the security computer systems at B&S Bank in the City - 3pm to midnight. He liked the hours, and the drive was acceptable most days. But by bus and train? Unthinkable until now.

Gavin had, in fact, ruled out the local buses. Or their timetables had ruled him out. So he had decided he would need to cycle the nine miles to the nearest railway station at Stansted Airport.

His need to leave work 30 minutes earlier than usual in order to catch the last train back had been tentatively cleared with his boss.

Would his boss sanction that for an extra three months? Would Gavin be able to handle it?

Anger won the battle inside his brain as Gavin looked around outside the court.

"Where is the bloody bus station, then? Better get used to this lark," he muttered to himself.

He found it and discovered he had a 20-minute wait until the next one to the railway station was due.

"Terrrrr-ific!"

Six months of this crap. It wasn't just the work commute which angered Gavin.

No transport on demand. No jumping into the car for a jaunt to the movies, a concert, a football game...or even to the supermarket. No ferrying Jim and Kate to their pals in an ever-increasing circle around Great Wilton.

How would Jim and Kate react when he informed them? Tough. They can get acquainted with their legs again.

He'd smoked two cigarettes and his anger had increased by the time the bus arrived.

He recognised two faces from the court also waiting in line. At least Gavin wasn't alone, it seemed.

A one-way fare to the railway station cost £1. He could have purchased a return for £1.40 but he didn't plan coming back that way.

Fortunately, he enjoyed a seat to himself on the bus as his mind rambled over the events in court.

Should he have got a brief? Should he have let rip against bloody speed cameras, trapping 'innocent' motorists who posed no threat to anyone, certainly not at the times Gavin travelled?

He'd had his day in court and, not surprisingly, the law of the land had won the day. Gavin actually felt quite kindly towards the Chief Magistrate. It wasn't that guy's fault; he was simply processing the law. It was the bloody law's fault.

Gavin had been caught speeding twice previously, five years ago when speed cameras first appeared on the motorway. He had successfully negotiated three further years of trouble-free driving and got a clean licence back.

Then the cameras returned.

Gavin had been flashed twice the previous January, shortly before the junction for Stansted Airport on the M11. Both flashes had jolted him. He was returning home from work at around one o'clock in the morning, music blaring away as usual and no other car in sight. He had ignored the 50mph speed limit while roadworks were in progress. Yes, more roadworks at the exact scene of his earlier offences.

The first police charge didn't teach Gavin his lesson. The second one a month later sent out warning bells.

Something inside of him triggered when he reached that spot and he obeyed the speed limit, absurd though it seemed at that time of night.

He was given no time to learn from his third 'crime'. He returned home from a brief trip abroad to find two NIPs awaiting his attention.

The Notices of Intended Prosecution informed the vehicle owner that his vehicle had been filmed breaking the speed limit. The vehicle owner was legally obliged to inform the authorities who was driving the vehicle at the time of the alleged offence.

Gavin was surprised. He couldn't recall any recent flashes? But these offences were not at his usual haunt.

Number three was again on the M11 but at a different location –

towards the end of the motorway, and the same spot where the first Mr Lucky in court had been trapped. It was dated June 27th at 2.20pm. Gavin would have been driving to work.

Number four – the serious one, the bad one, the feared one, the oh-my-god-I'm-going-to-be-banned one – was on the A120, the road taking Gavin home from the motorway.

It was dated July 3rd at 1.17am. Gavin would have been driving home from work.

"Jeeze," Gavin gasped. He didn't even realise there was a speed camera on the 120.

He had not spotted the sprouting of the cameras. There were more of them and in more locations. Gatsos were spreading across the nation like a very bad rash.

He had duly paid the fine for the third offence. He returned the fourth and waited, waited, waited for a court date.

Just as he had started hoping he may have escaped through some legal hole, the letter came. It was six months after his fourth offence and informed him he was due in court in two months.

He knew he was done for. He discussed his predicament with work colleagues and with mates down the pub. He was surprised to discover that many of his acquaintances had had brushes with the law.

But not one had been so incredibly stupid as to get flashed four times in six months, they cheerfully told him.

Though his stupidity irked him, Gavin felt a rising rage. He was righteously indignant at being branded, even though his offences were minor in the great scheme of things legal.

He didn't drink and drive, he didn't drive dangerously, he treated other road users with respect and was always alert in built-up areas. He was a father, for goodness sake.

He despised the lane-weavers who used motorways as their playground; he frowned upon the youngsters who burned rubber on his High Street; he had a positive loathing for truck drivers who took great delight in idling a matter of inches behind cars they believed were using their road space.

So, Gavin had a minor problem with speed. But did doing 56mph in a 40 zone at the dead of night really label him unfit to be allowed on the road?

No, Gavin insisted to himself. It bloody well did not.

The bus arrived at the station. A couple pushed past him and dashed towards the entrance.

A few minutes later, Gavin appreciated their haste. He had missed the London train while attempting to impress on the ticket-seller that he wanted a ticket to London which allowed him to return to Stansted Airport and not Harlow. He eventually understood the message that he would need two single tickets and the return to Stansted would have to be purchased in London.

After arriving on the platform to learn he had 28 minutes to kill before the next train, Gavin's mood was dark and menacing. It troubled him. He hadn't felt so bad in ages. It was as if he had been overtaken by a need to strike out, at what he wasn't sure. Revenge was in the air.

It was a long 28 minutes, but fruitful to Gavin. And by the time the train pulled into London's Liverpool Street station he had isolated the cause of his anger.

He wasn't mad at the court. He had to admit they'd treated him as fairly as their remit allowed. He wasn't mad at the police for prosecuting him. Only doing a job. It was their faceless allies that really annoyed him. The Gatsos – speed cameras – that he had discovered were assuming a key role nationwide in the fight against drivers.

Yes, Gavin knew now as an irrefutable fact of life that speed cameras were bad.

Speed Cameras Are Bad...Speed Cameras Are The Enemy...Speed Cameras Are Bad...he chanted to himself as he rather enjoyed the brisk 25-minute walk to the office.

Speed Cameras Are The Enemy.

And the world needed to wake up to that fact.

Gavin struggled through his shift, chanting away to himself from time to time. He drew sniggers and confused looks from colleagues.

He was still chanting as he strolled back to the railway station just in time to catch the last train back to Stansted. He then paid twelve quid for a cab home. This was turning out to be an expensive day. Yet his mood wasn't as dark as he would have thought.

He had decided a course of action and was determined to follow it through. He was so determined he slept unsoundly that night.

CHAPTER TWO

Soaring In Cyberspace

GAVIN had rarely needed an alarm clock. He shook himself up as soon as his eyes recognised a new day. Most of the time.

This day he was up like a shot, despite his restless night. He had things to do before he embarked on his lengthier journey to the office.

Breakfast was the customary fruit juice followed by coffee and cigarettes, usually taken standing in the kitchen of his four-bedroomed 1960s semi. Today he sat down at the kitchen table and started jotting down notes.

He was satisfied, grabbed a second coffee and powered up his computer in the adjacent room - his study, music, memorabilia and all-round junk room.

Gavin rattled off eight crisp paragraphs. Happy with his effort, he printed nine copies and placed one in a new folder, took out his favourite red felt-tipped pen and wrote GATSOS neatly across the top.

The remaining eight he stuffed into envelopes. Then he started searching for addresses in his telephone directories.

He addressed his important missive to three local newspapers, two Essex radio stations, the town council, his MP and the final one to the Chief Constable of Essex.

Gavin had written:

Dear sir/madam
I am writing to complain about the growing number of speed cam-

eras operating around the Essex area.

I have just been fined heavily and banned from driving for six months after being filmed breaking the speed limit on four occasions.

Of course, I admit I was wrong to speed. But do I really deserve to be banned from driving simply because I strayed a few miles per hour over the limit while travelling home from work in the early hours of the morning?

I was a menace to no-one. In fact, there was hardly anyone else travelling on the road at the same time as myself.

I could understand if the cameras were used to prevent people from driving like idiots close to built-up areas, or near hospitals or schools. But not to catch people on a virtually empty M11 at one o'clock in the morning.

Road safety? That doesn't wash. These cameras are there purely to trap motorists and rake in as much money as possible.

I am sure there are many other motorists who feel the same.

Speed cameras should be used sensibly, and not as an extra tax on decent motorists.

Yours Sincerely

Gavin Lloyd

Shortly before 9am he was dressed and stepping outside to send his letter on its way.

He hand-delivered those for the Wilton Advertiser and the council before heading for the Post Office to purchase several books of stamps. He would be needing them.

It was a pleasant mid-February day. "Good," thought Gavin. "I can bike it."

He had a couple of hours spare time, he reckoned, before he needed to leave for work. The commute would take care of his daily exercise, so once home Gavin slipped on a White Stripes CD and settled down with the morning paper.

He read the bits that took his eye, then managed to complete about two-thirds of the crossword. Not bad, he thought. In seven years of subscribing to The Daily Telegraph he had twice triumphantly completed the crossword. All by himself.

He still felt a little strange at having to shower and prepare for work two hours earlier than normal. But he had made what he considered the correct preparations even if the six-month ban still rankled him.

Before heading for court the previous day, he had driven his car into the garage – an event usually reserved for his annual vacation. He had taken his car key off his key ring and put it inside a wooden box on his bookshelves. No danger of absent-mindedly driving away and landing himself in hotter water.

"Let's see how you cope with being a car-free zone for a while," he told himself aloud as he showered.

Weather permitting, he intended to cycle to the railway station, catch the express train to London and walk the final two-and-a-bit miles to work.

He had made several test runs on his bicycle to Stansted Airport. There were two miles on the A120 but most of the eight-mile trip could be done along country lanes.

The by-pass helped make the old A120 less daunting for a casual cyclist like Gavin. The journey took him between 40 minutes (personal-best achieved one peaceful Sunday) and one hour and seven minutes (he had walked a while as the juggernauts roaring by had unnerved him).

He neatly folded his work clothes and put them in a plastic shopping bag. The plastic bag, his shoes, fluorescent waterproofs, cycle lights, puncture kit and a biography of some CIA veteran were then packed into his rucksack. It was a tight fit and made the rucksack quite heavy, but Gavin could handle it.

The bike ride wasn't too bad; the heavy traffic kept him alert on the main roads, as did a yapping dog as he meandered along the country lanes at a steady 13.5mph, according to his cycle computer clock.

Fifty minutes and 25 seconds after leaving home Gavin disembarked and chained up his Falcon cycle.

He bought a railpass which entitled him to a discount on the fare, but £11 a day was still twice as much as it would cost in petrol-money to get to work.

The trains ran efficiently every half hour, he had been informed by friends who worked at the airport. He had ten minutes to wait, so he could change into his work clothes in the gents rather than on the train.

He had forgotten how sweaty cycling usually made him. The tee-shirt underneath his fleecy top was soaked, the fleecy was damp at the back from pressing against the rucksack and his body.

"Hmmm, better bring a towel tomorrow," he thought. He managed to wash, dry himself down and dress just in time to catch the train. He didn't exactly feel like a million dollars, however.

He was unable to read much of the adventures of the CIA hero on the train, comfortable though the seats were.

Speed cameras kept popping into his head. Still, he had launched his plan by mailing his letters that morning.

Work was accompanied by more sniggers: his rucksack drew a range of unfunny quips and at one point he was ready to thump the next person who chortled "On yer bike!"

SCATE

There was a slight drizzle when he arrived back at Stansted, and it was colder than he expected.

He had changed into his cycling gear on the train and now donned his waterproofs over the top. He unchained his bike, fitted his lights and cycled home in 46 eerie minutes. The country lanes were dreadfully quiet. An occasional rustling noise made by some furry friend - he hoped friend - and the gentle whoosh of his wheels were all that he heard until a few cars flashed by him later on the main road.

Despite the chill of the night, the extra layer of waterproofing had left Gavin even sweatier by the time he arrived at his door.

"Time for another shower," he sighed.

During his regular hour of leisure before bed, Gavin sipped a large Jack Daniel's but struggled once more to get into the life of the CIA man. For the second night running he dozed off with speed cameras flashing through his brain.

The ride home on Thursday took place in heavier rain, driving into Gavin's face for several minutes. It was grand exercise, though, he jollied himself. And three days off now.

Gavin worked four regular shifts Monday-Thursday. The children stayed with him at the old family home on his days off.

Jim, a bright 15-year-old, was first to arrive from school. Gavin wanted to wait for his sister to join them before breaking the bad news.

Kate, two years younger, trooped in 15 minutes later.

"Well rascals, not sure how to put this...but your stupid dad has been banned from driving."

Jim had a half-smile on his face as he said: "Why? I thought you only had six points on your licence."

"I got another two last summer and was in court at Harlow on

Tuesday."

"Banned! You silly thing," laughed Kate.

"Oh! You can laugh!" said Gavin. "You are the last person to find it funny."

"Why?" she said, the laughter in her eyes less keen.

"Well think of all the driving you nag me to do. Sorry, but no more trips to pals for the next six months. But they're always welcome here."

"Waddya mean? Why can't you drive me to friends? I'm going to Bridget's tomorrow."

"Not in my car, you're not."

Kate looked puzzled.

"I'm banned...banned! B-A-N-N-E-D from driving, OK?"

"Oh, I though you just meant you were banned from driving to work."

Gavin laughed out loud. Kate was a little gem, if somewhat other-worldly at times.

They all enjoyed a good laugh as Gavin light-heartedly explained what had happened, his court appearance and his bike rides. "So, Jim, I don't exactly feel like a bike ride this weekend unless you insist."

Kate came to terms with her social predicament remarkably quickly. The news of dad's ban spread rapidly among her circle.

The following day Jim came into the kitchen to see how dinner was progressing.

"Whatcha listening to, dad?" he asked. "Thought you'd have the footie on?"

Gavin would normally have been listening to sport on BBC Radio 5 Live. But he'd been flicking through a couple of local stations just to check if there was any item about speed cameras. There hadn't been, so Gavin gave it up and switched stations.

He told Jim about his letter and sheepishly showed him the copy from his flimsy Gatso folder. He tried to explain his incredible, irritating annoyance, yet Jim was having a difficult time seeing his point of view. "But you WERE speeding, dad," he chipped in.

He told his son that he planned to write further letters, possibly even to the Prime Minister.

"Like he'll take any notice," said Jim. "You need a website."

Gavin's face lit up. "What a brilliant idea! I've been meaning to learn more about that kinda stuff. Fancy helping your old man again?"

"Sure," laughed Jim. "I'll keep it simple for you to start with."

Jim was a minor boffin in his father's eyes; self-taught, too, and seemingly very capable. Gavin was no Internet idiot, but he used it seldom: there were a few music sites he visited and he sometimes joined the children in online games. But he genuinely had been planning to learn more; he intended to keep abreast of his children's immersion in the techno-age.

Jim had helped his father get their new computer running three years previously. Their mother had taken the family one when she left Gavin and moved a mile across town. At that time personal computing was Greek to Gavin. He was a first-class operator on the security system at B&S Bank; having digested perfectly everything the instructor on his three-day course had delivered.

Yet he had struggled to get to grips with programmes, software, hardware, files and folders at home until he managed to persuade Jim he needed two hours of his patience.

He knew he would never be head-hunted by Microsoft, yet he felt like a pioneer as he and Jim sat down on the Sunday morning for the first lesson in becoming a webmaster.

Two hours later, the mystique had been stripped away and Gavin felt so pleased for himself and proud of his boy. He had had to ask Jim to explain the techno-babble on two occasions, but now he sat before his very own web page comprising a plain light-blue background, a headline which read 'Don't Ban Drivers...Ban Speed Cameras', a photograph of a Gatso which Jim had found somewhere, and, finally, the text of Gavin's letter.

As they carefully saved all dad's work in a desktop folder – again appropriately named Gatso – Jim rabbited on.

"Next weekend I'll show you how to make links and set up email and how to upload it and...oh, of course, you will need to purchase a domain. Thought of a good name?"

Gavin hadn't. "I'll give it some thought," he said. "Thanks, son."

"No problems, dad. Any chance of a fiver?"

Jim picked up his snooker cue, took the £5 offered by his dad and laughed as he wagged his finger at Gavin and said: "Just remember one thing, dad..."

"What?" asked Gavin.

"You WERE speeding."

Gavin smiled as he watched his whistling son bounce off to the snooker club.

Kate wasn't due back from a friend's for a few hours so Gavin planned to pop out to the local for a few pints.

Before getting ready, he sat down at the kitchen table. "Yes, a name," he mused.

His mind seemed a blank as he poised with pen and paper.

"Come on. Bloody think!" he muttered.

No grand thoughts would come. Just that chant returning: Speed

SCATE

Cameras Are Bad....Speed Cameras Are The Enemy...

He jotted down Speed Cameras Are Bad. Then S.C.A.B. Neat, he smiled to himself. But not quite appropriate.

The inner chanting continued. A few blank moments later, Speed Cameras Are The Enemy was scribbled on the paper. S.C.A.T.E. "YES! That's nice, real nice."

Though 20 years older than his son, Gavin had that jaunty teenage bounce about him as he left for the Dog And Duck.

The 'Dog' was fairly bouncy, too, when Gavin arrived. Sunday lunchtime was generally busy, more so when satellite TV was screening a big football game. Arsenal v Chelsea was thankfully nearing its goalless conclusion. Shame both of them couldn't lose, thought Gavin, a lifelong Manchester United supporter. In his defence, he always claimed he had been born eight miles from Old Trafford and made the occasional pilgrimage back.

"Hey! Speed king! How'd the court case go?" Ian greeted him.

"Cheers mate. Bitter would be nice. Thanks."

"Come on, come on. What d'yer get?"

"Six months. Couple hundred quid fine...plus costs. Bad day at Black Rock."

"Ha! You dozy bugger. That'll teach you."

Kevin joined them. "Hey! Was that you cycling along the 120 the other day? I did wave."

"Didn't see you, Kev. You know us supreme cyclists – always focused on the big 'uns."

A few offered commiserations, a few scoffed as expected as the news of Gavin's verdict passed round the pub.

The conversation turned to speed cameras. No-one spoke in their favour. Two newcomers to the village admitted they were both sitting on six points and were fearful of losing their licences, what with a speed camera on every street soon, they reckoned.

"Saw them putting another one on the Chelmsford Road last week," informed Mark. "Must be at least five on that stretch now."

"More of 'em in Southend than there are seashells," said Kevin.

"Almost ran up the backside of a van on the North Circular yesterday. Silly sod musta just rammed his brakes on when he saw the signs," said Sparky, an electrician with six points on his licence courtesy of the friendly Gatsos. "Wouldn't mind betting they cause more accidents than they prevent."

Sue Jenkins had been unusually quiet. She was blushing as she revealed: "I was flashed by one on the Chelmsford Road last weekend. What happens next?"

Gavin – by now the pub's dedicated expert – told her.

"First offence, is it?"

"Yes. But I daren't lose my licence. They seem to be everywhere all of a sudden. I heard on the news that more than a thousand were caught by one camera near Ipswich on a single day recently. We're supposed to watch out for other road users and pedestrians and kids and dogs, not these blasted things."

Gavin could well empathise with her indignation.

They chatted for a while. Gavin told her not to worry about three points, about his biking to the station and, as they walked home, about his letter.

Sue, a 30-year-old Gulf War widow who lived on the same street as Gavin, seemed mildly-amused as he poured out his dislike-bordering-on-hatred of all things speed camera-related. She commended him on his new hobby as they said their farewells.

Hobby? Gavin hadn't really thought of it as a hobby?

SCATE

Jim was back from the snooker club. He and dad chatted for a while. Gavin explained SCATE to him. Jim preferred SCAB but for once deferred to his father's judgment.

Gavin was tempted to ask Jim to get things up and running that evening but decided his son's homework must come first. Next weekend it would be – the launch of SCATE.

Two days later he answered his doorbell and was surprised to see Sue Jenkins there.

"Well it has arrived," she waved a letter at him. "You got a few minutes to spare?"

Gavin invited her in, made them both some coffee and they sat down in the kitchen to examine the Notice of Intended Prosecution.

Sue had indeed been caught travelling at a sprightly 55mph in a 40-zone on her way back from Chelmsford.

"Unless you plan to contest it, you're just going to have to cough up sixty quid and take three points on your licence," Gavin informed her. "Annoying isn't it?"

Sue groaned. "I'd just overtaken a lorry so I suppose I was going a bit nippy. And you say if I get four of these in three years I'll be banned?"

"Yes. So take it easy. Wish I'd heeded my own advice."

"You hear anything back from those folk you sent the letter to?"

"Well, yes, just the council so far. They claim it's nothing to do with them but thank you for your letter etc..."

Gavin took out his Gatso folder and showed Sue his original letter and the reply from the council. At least the council clerk's response had been quick.

As she was leaving Gavin told her about the planned website launch.

"Great! Let me know the link when it's online and I'll post a message."

"Post a message?" queried Gavin.

"On your message board. I assume it's going to be a forum-type site where people can have a good, old rant – even us WOMEN drivers."

"Oh, right."

"Good luck, and seriously do let me know how it goes. I think it's a great idea."

She handed him a card: "Here, my email address is on there. Bye."

"Cheers. Have a fun day...and watch your speed."

Sue turned and gave him a cheeky smirk as she trotted down the path.

Hmmm, a forum? The prospect intrigued Gavin. And he liked Sue from the little he knew of her. And she had seemed interested. And he hadn't really been sure where his hobby, idea, scheme – whatever you wish to call it – was taking him. He was simply letting off steam. Now he realised others like Sue wanted to have their say, too. Even WOMEN drivers.

Gavin struggled through the week. He was forced to leave his bike at home one day and fork out for taxis owing to an accurate weather forecast. He had never dressed and undressed so often, and he had travelled by train more times in the last few days than in the previous dozen or so years.

He had to admit, however, that he didn't miss his car as much as he had expected. Only five months and three weeks to go.

He couldn't wait for the children to arrive after school so Jim could give him his next lesson in webmastery.

He had received one more reply to his letter, from Essex Police. Basically, the Chief Constable thanked Gavin for his letter and had

SCATE

noted its contents.

"Hi dad," Kate breezed in. "I'm staying over at Amy's tonight, if that's all right."

A statement rather than a request.

"Kerry's mum will take us and Amy's dad will bring us back tomorrow. As you're banned!"

She gave Gavin a frown becoming a Victorian schoolmistress. He was pleased she was taking the situation with good humour.

"Gotta dash," she gave Gavin a kiss on the cheek. "Being picked up at mum's as my clothes are there. Jim has something from mum for you."

"From mum? What?"

"Dunno, something about nutters who drive too fast."

Jim arrived with a groan as he threw down two heavy bags containing some schoolwork and his weekend clothes.

"You owe me £12.34, dad," was his greeting of choice.

"Hi, son. What for?"

"Well you owe me and I owe mum 'cos I used her card to buy scate.co.uk for you. Hope that's OK?"

"Wow! Fantastic," beamed Gavin.

"We can have a look at it tomorrow morning, all right? Going out to the snooker club tonight.

"Oh and mum cut this out of the evening paper," Jim handed his dad a letters' page. Mum's yellow marker had highlighted one midway down the page. The headline above Gavin's letter read: 'Speed Cameras: Good or Bad?' Rather neutral, thought Gavin as he flicked through the article and noted that they had at least published his letter in its entirety, and included his name and address.

"Got much response yet?" asked Jim.

Gavin told him and informed him of Sue's NIP.

"She doesn't look the speeding type."

"Oh and pray tell what does the speeding type look like? Does your father look like the speeding type?"

Jim smiled: "You know what I mean. Boy racers and all."

Gavin also revealed Sue's comments about a message board.

Jim looked up. "Adventurous, huh. I thought this was just for you to have a blast at the cops? I can't do boards myself but..."

Jim went into a barrage of techno details which baffled Gavin. But he got the gist, yes no problems with having a forum on the SCATE site.

"Tomorrow morning, eh dad? Early if you like as I'm going out in the afternoon. What's for dinner? I'm famished. Lemme get this bloody homework out of the way."

An hour later, the Wilton Advertiser popped through the letterbox. Packed with adverts for expensive houses, cars and services, the Advertiser had a smattering of local news, sports results, school galas and the like; and a letters' page.

Gavin hurriedly found his page. The main letter was a governor highlighting concerns of over-crowding at the local junior school, which Gavin's children had attended. But given considerable prominence was Gavin's epic; again every single word was printed. The headline was an improvement in Gavin's opinion: 'Put Speed Cameras Where They Are Needed.'

After Jim returned from the snooker club, he and dad watched TV for an hour and Gavin was about to pop up to the 'Dog' for the last hour when the phone rang.

An unfamiliar voice asked if he was 'Gavin Lloyd'.

"Yes," said Gavin thinking this was rather late for anyone flogging windows or bathroom suites. "Who is this?"

"My name's John. Read your letter in the paper. Very interesting."

"Thanks," interrupted Gavin and told John to watch out for the imminent launch of the SCATE website.

"Sounds great," said John. "Heard a few things about you. You're not alone. There's a meeting being set up. Have a think if you wanna join us. I'll be in touch. G'night."

The phone went dead. Not alone? Meeting? Wanna join us? Gavin was intrigued.

He dialled 1471. A voice told him: "You were called today at 9.56pm. I am sorry we do not have the caller's number."

CHAPTER THREE

A Trumped-Up Vandal

The tuneless humming of the theme from Dr Who wafted through the smoky room.

"So, boys and girls, who and what are we exactly looking for?" boomed the sergeant, bringing his class to attention.

"A fruitcase who lives in a Tardis," quipped DC Jamieson, stubbing out his cigarette in his coffee cup and binning the offending item.

"Very funny," snapped back DS Abrahams, eyeing five others among his eight boys and girls who followed Jamieson's lead and ditched their fags.

"And let me assure you all, myself and the Super share your good humour. So much so that all unbooked leave is suspended for the next fortnight. A resounding pat on the back is on offer from the Super for the head of a certain Dr Glue. Our beloved Super did not specify whether or not he wanted the head attached to the body." DS Abrahams let his comments sink in before reading from notes.

"Here it is so far then. And very thin reading it makes, too.

"Someone calling himself Dr Glue – we are assuming male for now – had a very busy evening on February 26-27th. Between the hours of approximately 9.20pm and 3.40am he managed to knock out nine speed cameras, four here, two in Liverpool, one in Manchester, one in Cheshire and finally one in Cumbria. Seven were on motorways and the other two on A roads.

"Based on initial reports and timings from the traffic units we believe he operated south-to-north. Do not assume this is any indication of where this bugger may live.

"Some of you will be aware that he stuck strong, plastic plates over the cameras. These are picnic plates readily available at many outlets. The patterns on them varied. So no clues there."

"Plenty of glue, though," giggled DC Havens.

"Yes, Havens! Plenty of bloody glue. Thank you for bringing me onto the matter of the glue in your customary hilarious style.

"Plenty of bloody VERY STRONG glue, in fact. A stronger type of glue than you will find at your local store. A generic make, so no clues on the glue sellers."

He stared at Havens, who stifled a boyish smile.

"We do, however, know that this glue is imported from the Far East and then processed by at least 37 firms in the UK. It is particularly favoured by those involved in heavy-duty carpentry. Havens, as my favoured son of the day, you will investigate the glue angle.

"The rest of you, any thoughts so far?"

Before anyone had a chance to speak, DS Abrahams rattled off some figures; no wonder the Super was raging. Dr Glue's antics had cost Lancashire Constabulary alone 95 wasted police hours on February 27th, taken maintenance man cheery Joe away from other essential work, cost the force a staggering £120,000 a day in lost revenue – not to mention the funds needed to replace the damned things.

The over-burdened forensics department was clocking up overtime at a rate which disturbed the Super. Four other forces were involved, with similar costs and concerns.

Abrahams fell silent.

"Sounds like we're looking for someone who's recently been nailed by a Gatso," suggested DC Pollock.

Abrahams rolled his eyes. "Fair comment, Pollock. But I have no need to remind this room how many speedsters we grab on camera every week on our patch. Dr Glue vandalised equipment over a 95-mile stretch of road, and even managed a couple of detours."

"What about other cases, boss?" said DC Smith. "I recall reading that two blokes in South Wales were jailed for setting fire to one. Maybe they know Dr Glue?"

Abrahams was fully aware that there had been sporadic attacks against speed cameras across the land. Most cases involved angry motorists taking their anger out on the cameras with whatever tool they had handy. Minor damage here and there. Others had been more determined, setting aflame petrol-filled tyres placed over Gatsos; or driving into them; or hacking them down with chainsaws. Even one case of a camera being uprooted lock, stock and barrel and put in a field next to a scarecrow.

All appeared isolated incidents, however. Nothing approached the scale of Dr Glue's night on the roads. Abrahams agreed with his chief that there was something more sinister about this wave of attacks.

"We have been in contact with several other forces, Smith. No joy to report, I'm afraid. Though inquiries are on-going."

Quiet reigned. Abrahams could not blame the roomful of experienced detectives for their silence. Like him, they had little to go on.

He went over the information they had – the glue, the calling card, the locations – before assigning duties. He pinned up notes and stressed the urgency with which Superintendent Charleston wanted this matter brought to a successful conclusion. He left behind a group of officers scratching their collective head.

"Eight officers assigned to nail a trumped-up vandal?" DC Smith voiced her concern to a pair of colleagues.

"It's not the crime or the criminal," retorted Jamieson. "It's the money. And the Super's scared shitless that Dr Glue will be back."

Superintendent Eric Charleston was indeed worried about the money. His Chief Constable was even more worried and had vented his fury in Charleston's presence. The Super took it personally and the message went down the line.

Forty-eight hours after the hunt for Dr Glue had begun in earnest, DC Smith reported back to DS Abrahams.

"Sir, I've got a possible lead on our doctor."

"Really? Let's have it then," said an interested Abrahams whose only fresh information had concerned the business card – home-printed, Epson paper and probably on one of 16 makes of printer of which thousands had been sold in the UK.

Helen Smith told Abrahams about her sighting of Dr Glue.

"I was surfing last night and decided to key Dr Glue into a search engine and BINGO!"

When Abrahams had persuaded Smith to calm down and explain to him in simple terms, he discovered that she had stumbled across their target on an Internet website run by the SCATE organisation.

Abrahams had never heard of SCATE, was slightly amused by the acronym and almost begged Smith for more information.

"Well, sir, it was quite late last night when I discovered someone going by the handle Dr Glue on the forums at SCATE. I had a browse for about ten minutes, but as I said it was late and as you know me and DC Pollock are due to meet Merseyside Police in Liverpool today. Do you want me to look into the SCATE connection further?"

Abrahams did not need much persuading. This was the only lead they had.

"Yes, Helen," he said, clearly happy as he rarely called officers by their first names. "I am sure Pollock can get to Liverpool and back without anyone holding his hand.

"Good luck. And keep me informed of everything."

SCATE had come a long way since wriggling out of Gavin Lloyd's brain the previous year.

Jim had helped dad launch it successfully. Gavin had devoured books and magazines and internet articles on web design. He was deep into the techno-age by now. The CIA man's history was gathering dust on a shelf.

The message boards were proving a roaring success. Gavin, with Jim's help, naturally, had managed to incorporate them courtesy of free software providers about six weeks after the site-launch. Gavin had posted the first message: 'This is a test.'

Sue Jenkins had been the first sign-up and posted a funny three-verse poem about the Fatsos getting fatter on Gatsos.

The treasury loved them, so did the transport department. The police was split on the issue, though most saw the advantages in cash terms as more bodies were taken off road duty. Insurance companies were split, too. Some added small premiums to drivers convicted of speeding, while some did try to ride the storm. The manufacturers were overjoyed, as was the workforce who eagerly snapped up the regular offer of overtime.

Sue was a key figure in SCATE, was often around the Lloyd household and Jim and Kate scented romance in the air.

Gavin had wanted to invite Sue along to his meeting with Humphrey Bellow and Samuel Owens, but he reluctantly decided to go alone.

Just a few hours after DC Smith had reported her news of Dr Glue to DS Abrahams, 200 miles away Gavin walked into Conservative Party offices at Frowstone for his meeting with his MP and the Tory

Party leader. Even though he was a lifelong Labour voter, Gavin was grateful for the support of the Right Honourable Humphrey Bellow, MP for Frowstone and surrounding areas.

Bellow had replied to his letter in due course, and provided a lengthy response, which expressed sympathy with Gavin's concerns. Two other constituents, it transpired, had written to Bellow complaining about speed cameras.

Gavin had met Bellow briefly on one of his occasional forays into Great Wilton, and they had exchanged correspondence. Yet Gavin was still unsure whether his MP was a real-life opponent of speed cameras or simply seizing an opportunity to attack the Government.

His 25-minute meeting with Bellow and Samuel Owens won him over.

Owens seemed much more sincere in the flesh than he did on TV. Both he and Bellow listened intently as Gavin explained for a few minutes how SCATE had come about and what it was about.

They nodded and issued noises of approval as Gavin explained that speed cameras were good business for the police – a £150m-a-year business. A motorist was caught speeding every 13 seconds in the UK. The Government projected a no-nonsense message that *safety* cameras (not speed cameras, they insisted) were essential in the fight to make Britain's roads safer for the people. But many motoring experts and organisations disagreed.

Gavin bombarded them with statistics. Did they realise that road accidents were increasing probably BECAUSE of speed cameras not in spite of them? Were they aware that many motoring experts challenged the Transport Department's proclamations on speed?

He told them that he and his members at SCATE believed police should concentrate on apprehending dangerous and drunk drivers;

that speed cameras should be restricted to deployment in populated areas and by schools and hospitals. He cited cases from the SCATE forums:

The guy fined for speeding while taking his wife to hospital. She gave birth to their first child six minutes after arriving.

The grandmother with a 40-year clean licence who was flashed doing 36mph in a 30 zone.

Cases like Gavin's own: drivers being caught speeding on deserted roads.

He stressed that SCATE didn't condone speeding but wanted sensible traffic policing, and claimed that old-fashioned traffic police would never have dreamed of charging those involved in the cases he'd related.

The two Tories were definitely in accord with Gavin and discussed their aims and policies. They pledged a future Tory Government to restoring commonsense on British roads.

They would be delighted to work hand-in-hand with SCATE. They could not, however, risk having their party's good name attached to any organisation which operated outside the law.

They were impressed by the peaceful protests organised by SCATE, so could Gavin provide assurances that neither he nor any of his members were involved in nor supported any of the publicised criminal attacks against speed cameras?

Gavin most certainly could.

Samuel Owens had two schools, a library and an old person's home to visit so he promised to keep in touch with Gavin via Humphrey Bellow and his transport spokeswoman, Caroline Mitchell.

They all shook hands and wished each other well.

What would his old man think? His son shaking hands with the

Tory Party leader!

Gavin was sure his late father would have understood and, in fact, been quite proud of his one and only.

He couldn't wait to get back to Great Wilton and report on his meeting to Sue and the others.

Naturally, he watched his speed as he drove the 20 miles home. He'd been back on the road six months and his licence was Persil clean.

While Gavin was becoming something of an authority on speed cameras, cars were a different matter. He was never one to waste a weekend with his head under the bonnet. His four-year-old Mondeo 1.6 was a vehicle to get him from A to B. There was another car waiting on his drive as he carefully parked his Mondeo next to it.

J.J.'s black BMW 317i convertible befitted its owner – moderately flash.

John Jacobs was a 32-year-old scrap dealer who moved out of his native East End to Romford, an Essex town a few miles south of Great Wilton. He looked and occasionally acted more like a rock star; his thick mane of blond hair resting on his pin-striped suit made him stand out in any crowd.

He had been sitting on nine points for 15 months. If he was a careful driver, six would be wiped off his licence within the year. The other three points would disappear soon afterwards. It hadn't been easy for him, though. Despite his natural easy-come-easy-go nature, like Gavin he had been so incensed by his 'crimes' to want to do something about them.

He had become a good friend of the Lloyd household, sharing a passion for snooker with Jim. The Romford snooker halls were the only organisations J. J. had ever signed up for – until SCATE was born.

SCATE

Gavin met him on the pathway.

"Wotcha Gav. Just dropped some stuff off through your door, cuttings from the Romford rags and one or two from the Evening Standard. How'd the meeting go?"

Gavin gave him a quick resume and asked if he would be back later for the meeting.

"Sure. Just on my way to Saffron Walden to arrange a deal. Cash, of course," he winked and was on his way.

"Irrepressible as ever," tutted Gavin as he unlocked his door.

Gavin worked from home these days. SCATE had been taking up so much time that he decided to make it his full-time job - so much for being just a new hobby – and managed to eke out a living, though he was quite well down on his B&S salary.

Small donations came in from site visitors, a few larger ones from mainly anonymous sources in the motor trade. He also had earnings from a growing number of articles he had penned. He was currently working on one for a Toronto-based magazine; the Canadians had had very unpopular trials with speed cameras.

Website advertisements yielded a modest monthly sum. He had links to motoring periodicals, accessory sites and a growing batch of manufacturers of equipment designed to fool or block the speed cameras.

Jamming devices had been deemed illegal, but the entrepreneurs would not be cowed, so out came a host of machines to enable the motorist to stay one step ahead of the police.

State-of-the-art laser, radar and satellite technology was used to produce software packages that would alert drivers when they were approaching speed cameras. People seemed happy to pay to keep their licences clean.

Scate.co.uk even had its own databases, some run by Gavin and others via users. These informed site visitors of the location of every known speed camera in the UK. Gavin found this the most time-consuming aspect of his webmastery, but the one that was most popular, judging by the number of hits on those pages.

A few weeks earlier, Gavin had uploaded a stunning interactive map of the UK. An acquaintance of J.J.'s had produced it – for cash, of course. Visitors could zoom in to regions, counties or even their own tiny villages to discover the exact location of cameras. To date, the map revealed details of 9,000 cameras, and the rate was growing.

Gavin would update the database later. For now he wanted to check his mail and prepare his notes on the meeting with Samuel Owens and Humphrey Bellow.

He put the parcel from J.J. to one side and mock-snarled as he tossed a couple of bills into a tray.

He moved to his computer and just started typing, from memory, a report for the site on his meeting with the Tory two when his SCATE phone rang.

Kate called it his Bat-phone, but the second and third lines had become essential to Gavin to keep his personal and 'hobby' interests separate.

Gavin didn't recognise the number calling so he adopted his businesslike manner:

"Scate. How can we help you?"

"I'd like to speak to Gavin Lloyd, please," answered the unfamiliar female voice.

"I'm Gavin. Who's speaking, please?"

"Hello Mr Lloyd. My name is Helen Smith and I'm a detective constable with Lancashire police. I have a few questions I'd like to ask you." Lancashire police? Gavin hadn't been back north in ages. What could they want with him?

"Ermm, sure. Fire away."

"You are the webmaster of scate.co.uk. Is that correct?"

"Yes," he replied. He was tempted to say 'of course it is you cretin and that's where you found this phone number' but he went along with the formality. "How can I help you?"

"We have good reason to believe that one of your members has committed a criminal offence, several offences actually. I'd like you to tell me everything you know about someone who goes by the name of Dr Glue."

DC Smith purposely avoided suggesting whether the suspect was male or female.

"Dr Glue? Hmm. Dr Glue?" murmured Gavin. "I've never heard any of our members use that name. What exactly are these offences you mentioned?"

DC Smith didn't answer his question. Her voice became a notch harsher: "Well I am sure you are aware of Dr Glue, a regular poster of messages at the forums on your site. I have noticed at least 17 in the last three weeks. And you are telling me you don't know this person?"

"Oh! A forum user!" said Gavin. "We have hundreds of those. Doesn't mean they are members of SCATE, though."

"Explain, please. From what I can see Dr Glue is a site regular," said DC Smith curtly.

"Well, there are a handful of members – people who help me with the admin etc. But anyone can use the forums; all they need is a valid email address. I insist on that so I can block people who abuse the site. And, of course, you will have seen our disclaimer regarding illegal activites."

"You're telling me anyone can leave notes on your site and you don't have an inkling who they are?" DC Smith sounded incredulous.

Gavin wasn't happy with the frostiness developing in the exchange.

"Of course! That's the beauty of the Internet – anonymity and protection. But, as I already said, I block those who post abusive or actionable notes. We have hundreds of users and it is physically impossible for me to read all the posts. So generally I wait for others to email me about any loonies posting, and I deal with it. What has this guy done?"

"So you're saying that the only information you have on Dr Glue is an email address?"

"Yes," said Gavin, getting annoyed that this copper wouldn't enlighten him on the reason for her call.

"Can I have it, then?"

Gavin quickly made up some techno-gibberish about the user details being on a computer which was busy uploading large files and he would not be able to access it for maybe two to three hours.

"Can I take your number please and I'll get back to you later today or first thing tomorrow morning?"

"As soon as possible, please," said DC Smith and gave Gavin a number to call.

"Will do, and can you please tell me what this Dr Glue has..."

DC Smith had rung off before Gavin had time to finish his question.

Strange call. Surly copper. Gavin dashed over to his SCATE computer, a new, very expensive model with a huge 160 gigabyte hard drive. It was permanently connected to scate.co.uk thanks to the recently-installed cable network in this Essex outpost.

He searched scate for Dr Glue and a file came up promptly. It revealed that Dr Glue had been a user for just over a month, had posted a total of 29 messages in three separate forums. Not an unusually heavy user.

The private scate log file revealed that Dr Glue had signed up using the email address: DrGlue666@yahoo.com.

Gavin hadn't told the Lancashire cop that users were also invited to include personal details in their profile, for public view or just for the good folk at scate.co.uk's research.

Gavin discovered that Dr Glue was a 27-year-old female who taught classics at Balliol College, Oxford. She had a Phd from St Andrews, Edinburgh. She had five kids. She liked cats, hated antelopes. Her favourite colour was dark black, her fave music South American samba. She supported Plymouth Argyle. Her politics were none-of-your-fuckin-business but I suppose a soft, speckled turquoise. She drove a 1960s London bus.

The webmaster laughed out loud. He really should read some of these profiles more regularly.

He wanted to phone DC Smith immediately with the joyous news.

He resisted temptation and instead made some more coffee and settled down to examine Dr Glue's posts. He glanced through them for a while and noticed nothing remarkable or contentious in the content. A few phrases struck him as odd, though. Gavin made a mental note to return to Dr Glue but time was flying today and he needed to write his report and finish some admin before Jim and Kate arrived. They were spending a week with each parent these days.

He'd just finished loading his 300-word report on a promising meeting with the Tory hierarchy to the front page of the SCATE site when the children crashed into his peace within ten minutes of each other. He proudly showed them the front page, complete with a photo of dad and Samuel Owens, snapped by Humphrey Bellow on Gavin's trusty Canon digital camera.

Jim knew who Samuel Owens was, Kate said: "Oh, I've seen him on the telly. Talks a lot. Borrrring! I'm starving." She began raiding the fridge. Jim and Kate had perpetual hunger in common. Kate was snacker-in-chief, considering lunch at school a valuable waste of gossip time.

"Hey, careful in there! We've a meeting tonight and I'd really like some of that food saving for our guests. In fact, you're welcome to help me make the sandwiches."

J.J. was the first to arrive, fresh from the successful conclusion of his deal. He jested with Jim and Kate while awaiting the others.

The meetings were held whenever possible, which usually meant when Frank McIvor was in the area.

The only flash thing about McIvor was the personalised plate on his Range Rover FM 1964, the year of his birth. Otherwise, he was a totally different character to J.J.

He split his time between his hometown Dundee and the London area where he sold much of his Scottish premium malt whisky. He always brought Gavin some samples when he came to visit.

Today yielded three bottles: Balvenie, Royal Lochnagar and Macallan from the eastern highlands – quality beyond Gavin's personal budget, though he had in the past treated himself at Christmas.

"Cheers! To all our good friends north of the border," said Gavin as he gently laid the bottles in his cabinet. The meetings were teetotal. All had agreed this was fair on the drivers, and the last thing they wanted was a SCATE founder member on a drink-drive charge.

Like Gavin, Frank McIvor was of average build and height. Unlike the cleancut Gavin, McIvor sported an awesome brownish moustache whose thickness varied weekly.

His driving ban had ended ten months ago. Just two flashes had nailed him. He was banned for steaming back to Dundee up the A1 at 110mph. It had been 3am and no other car in sight. Gavin had heard many a similar story to his own. McIvor had employed a chauffeur to see him through the dark days, as he called his ban, but was now back behind the wheel. He kept on the right side of the law by breaking up his journey home instead of driving through the night, as he would have preferred.

So he was at Gavin's, then would head north for a few hours at a Newcastle motel before an early morning sales meeting. Still, he would be inside the sanctity of Dundee by mid-day.

Sue Jenkins arrived to warm greetings, especially from flirtatious Frank who once again insisted on trying to find her ticklish bits with his moustache.

Neil Proust arrived to complete the quintet of SCATE founders. Gavin's doorway was barely wide enough to allow the beefy Yorkshireman into the house. The 41-year-old truck driver from Leeds had piled on the pounds since his days fighting for the Crown. None of the members was quite sure which branch of the Special Forces had employed Proust's skills, but he had once shown them medals from numerous skirmishes around the globe.

He did regular runs down from Yorkshire to northern Europe, usually taking the Harwich-Hook Of Holland ferry. He never failed to drop by Gavin's on his way home.

"Better get a move on with this meeting, then, lads and lass. Gotta a bunch of starving illegals in the truck," he quipped.

Proust had a clean licence. He had contacted Gavin after seeing his letter in a newspaper while he was waiting to board a ferry at Harwich. He was still grieving the loss of his best friend, a veteran from their army days who had hung himself after losing his licence. His final straw had been a speed camera that cost him his job and his livelihood with the same firm. He left behind a widow, two young kids and considerable debts.

They nibbled the sandwiches and sipped tea as Gavin opened proceedings by relating his meeting that day. They toasted the success of the site map and a couple of recent feature articles in the quality Sunday papers before each member delivered a report.

Frank McIvor had been organising demos in Scotland, originating in Dundee and quickly spreading to the main cities, Aberdeen, Edinburgh and Glasgow.

The first, five months ago, hadn't held out much hope as a handful of disgruntled motorists turned up to hang around a Gatso on the approach to Dundee. It had been a farce. They simply stood around and chatted among themselves for three hours, sympathising with each other's plight at the hands of the law. Occasionally they would jump up and point at the speed camera to alert bewildered drivers passing by.

The chaos was more organised these days. But the police had become involved at one demo when 200-plus supporters turned up at two spots on the A68, reported McIvor.

The protesters were well behaved, just waving their placards as well as handing out leaflets at petrol stations and pubs.

"I was shocked when a couple of coppers turned up and told me the placards were being used to deliberately cover the cameras," insisted McIvor, a glint in his eye but his palms held open in disbelief.

"They claimed we were guilty of obstruction. I told 'em to sod off as we had a legitimate right to protest. They made vague threatening noises about arrests but I could sense their hearts weren't in it.

"We all went for some tea and returned for another hour after the cops had left. Couple days later I got this note from a local sergeant. I replied saying I was only prepared to deal with the Chief Constable...or maybe a superintendent if I was in a good mood."

Laughter around Gavin's dining room table.

"Here's a disc with some nice photos on it. Some of the homemade placards are funny – look good on the site."

"Interesting point about the police, Frank. Can they arrest people?" said Gavin.

"Technically, I think they could," chipped in J.J. "But I don't think they'd dare – just make 'emselves look more bleedin' stupid."

"Don't overestimate the intelligence of the Scottish police," said deadpan McIvor to more laughter.

"...which brings be nicely onto my little piece of research on the forces of evil," said J.J. "Seems PC Plod is all over the bleedin' place.

"I've been reading all those heavy kinda papers that Gavin here has a preference for," J.J. was no idiot but liked to put on the East End thickie act for an audience. "Plus some mates up and down the land have sent me emails and scans and cuttings....

"And, well, the cops can't make up their own tiny minds. Here's a disc with the collected ramblings of 12 Chief Constables. Five of 'em think the Gatsos are the greatest gift to the British police force since the invention of the truncheon. Two of 'em are straddling that fence so firmly it must ache rotten. Two, yes just two for now, are so anti I commend them for honorary SCATE membership. And the other three are swaying ever so slightly towards the pro lobby but are very worried about the public backlash from motorists and decreasing confidence in their officers. Hoping to get more comments from our leading cops in the near future.

"I've done my best with it but maybe one of you wordsmiths could knock it into shape."

With that, J.J. gave way to Neil Proust.

"Well your comrades in the north have been busy," said Proust, and blushingly added: "I had a run-in with one the other day. Honestly, hand on heart it was a total accident. Well, almost.

"I was in this lay-by having ten minutes kip. This idiot in a Rover parked right in front of me so I had to reverse to get out. I heard this bang and realised I'd hit something; didn't realise it was a Gatso at first, honest! When I did, I just couldn't resist edging back another yard. You wouldn't believe how easily it keeled over."

All just stared at Proust until they saw Gavin coughing into his handkerchief, clearly unable to control a giggling fit. It was infectious and within seconds the group around the table were roaring with laughter.

Proust just blushed more. His dry "No-one saw me, I'm sure," merely served to herald a fresh outburst of school ground giggles.

When eyes had been dried and composures regained, Gavin adopted the solemnity of a judge.

"Dear me, Neil. You should be on the stage. Seriously, though, come on...we all know we can't get into that sort of stuff."

The table nodded in approval, but heads remained bowed as if in fear of eye contact prompting more laughing fits.

Proust managed to complete a few scattered crumbs of information about petitions at service stations along the M62, which linked the east and west coasts. A series of letters to the large evening papers of Manchester, Liverpool and Sheffield had led to bulging mailbags and heated exchanges on the letters pages. He noted that the mass-media and tabloid Press, in particular, had shown little interest in the subject so far. Maybe this was something worth exploring. He was relieved to hand the baton to Sue Jenkins.

Typical of Proust, honest as the day is long, thought Sue as she struggled to keep a straight face while informing the group of her recent activities. Sue was probably the key person in keeping SCATE in a reasonably well-organised state.

If Gavin was the de facto chairman, Sue was chief executive – and secretary, liaison officer and, generally, the best thing a group like SCATE could have.

She had roped in some free legal experts. Their composite pages on the legal aspects of Gatsos were popular on the SCATE site and a classic example of plain English. One of them had defended for free a London mother and helped her escape a fine.

The meeting closed with customary personal chit-chat: How's the wife? Kids? Dog? Need a new striker, don't they? Then the travellers were on their way.

Gavin whispered to Sue if she'd like to stay behind for a nightcap. She often did.

He had fought to keep a tight grip on his tongue during the meeting; now he was desperate to quiz Sue.

"What do you know about a Dr Glue?" he probed as he poured two large Balvenies.

Christ, I sound like a Lancashire copper, he thought.

"Glue? Dr Glue?" Sue shook her head. "No idea. Who is he?" Gavin told her the details – or what scant details he knew following his interview with DC Smith. Then he showed her Dr Glue's site profile and a few posts.

"Obviously a bloke," said Sue. "What's he done?"

"No idea. Ever-so friendly DC Smith wouldn't tell me though I did ask a couple of times. How d'yer know it's a bloke? Been trying to think, but I am sure she never said Dr Glue was a he or she."

"Well, no member of my fair sex would find that 'turquoise' crap as funny as you men do."

"Do you think I should help the police? I could give them the email address but it is obviously fictitious."

"Tricky...I rather enjoy our middle way with the cops."

"Wish she'd told me what they wanted him for. I mean, he could be a murderer, a robber, rapist – or what if he's done something to children?"

"Come on, Gavin. Would they really make a check phone call to us if they were chasing Public Enemy Number One? I'd guess it's some geezer who's torched a Gatso on the leafy lanes of Lancashire...oh, wasn't Neil funny? One of the toughest blokes in the world, embarrassed at knocking one over. Accidentally, of course."

Another moment of mild mirth ensued before Gavin spoke again: "I think I'll insist the miserable cow tells me what it's all about before I offer any assistance."

"Sounds fair enough to me. I'm sure if they wanted to push it legally they need warrants and some better information linking us to Dr Glue than a few posts on our boards. Do you have any idea who he is?"

By now, Dr Glue was firmly established as a BLOKE by the SCATE neighbours.

"No," replied Gavin, truthfully. "Something did strike me as odd, though. All his posts are in perfect English, you what I mean; none of the common Net shorthand. Who writes like that ALL the time?

Our police 'guests', journos, professional people?"

"Well SHE is a prof at some posh uni," Sue winked.

"But I noticed the headers on his posts were more, errm, street-speak, you know? And they bear no relation to his topic."

Gavin walked Sue back to the PC and explained what he was talking about.

"Look at this one 'Stick With Me, Man', and this one here 'Glue's Sorry Now?' and his latest one, yesterday, 'Stuck It Up 'Em Last Night'. Then he just writes about anything. About stories in the Press, Government announcements, that kinda stuff. The last one was just a list of stats: how many people were done by Gatsos last year in relation to the number of unsolved serious crimes. Not sure of the logic of his argument but puzzled, definitely puzzled by the header."

"I've got it!" Sue waved her right hand, while her left mimicked a man smoking a pipe. "We're looking for an educated, middle-aged chap whose kids listen to too much Eminem. Quick! To Scotland Yard!"

"I'm just intrigued, that's all. The copper's attitude struck a strange chord."

"Sorry, Gavin. You know me, try to look on the bright side." Sue did. But Gavin guessed some of it was forced.

The shortish, tidy brunette had rapidly come to terms with widowhood. Some claimed she did not mourn the loss of her husband too deeply as he had been 'a bit of a bastard' towards her.

Her speeding fine caused her more worry. Since then, she and Gavin had grown closer and closer. They worked well together, enjoyed the occasional friendly date or dinner at either one's home; they were close enough to poke fun at each other. Gavin had consid-

-ered if she'd be keen on the next step, but bade his time. Why ruin a good thing?

"So whatcha gonna do, then?"

"Well, as we said, I'll ask her to tell me what it's all about before I offer any info. I'll adopt my official tone," he said gravely.

"Great. Make it early, eh? Mind if I come round and earwig? Need to be at work by ten."

"Sure," said Gavin. "Anytime after 8.30. Kids'll be on their way to school by then."

Sue collected her coat and pecked Gavin on the cheek. "Night. I'll be back for breakfast."

Gavin watched over her as she walked the few yards home.

CHAPTER FOUR

Royals Off The Front Page

Helen Smith had not been idle since speaking with Gavin Lloyd. Nor had her colleagues.

They'd checked police databases, the substance importers, glue manufacturers to see if they ever branded a product called Dr Glue; they'd been through the yellow pages of many of the big towns close to where the villain had struck; they'd discovered there were hundreds of thousands of plastic picnic plates available in the UK.

The only lead they had was DC Smith's website contact. It looked promising.

The Super had been informed by DS Abrahams and was keeping his fingers crossed. Despite the chief's anxiety that Dr Glue could strike again, the Super realised he could not afford to keep such a large team working on this case as long as desired. He planned to give them until after the weekend before releasing at least three of them for other duties.

Sue Jenkins had helped Gavin set her up by another telephone, with a tape-machine attached to it. They felt conspiratorial. Both were now desperate to discover the nature of the police interest in their forum user.

"Right," said Gavin. "I'll ring her now. Be best to call her before she calls me; it will make it look as though we are being helpful. Give us an edge."

DC Smith had left the fruitless morning briefing and was preparing to ring the webmaster when her phone rang.

"Detective Smith?"

"Yes. This is DC Smith."

"Hello, this is Gavin Lloyd. We spoke yesterday afternoon..."

"Yes. Thanks for calling Mr Lloyd. Do you have the information I asked for?"

"Well, of course we'd like to help the police but we really do need to know what this is all about. What are you saying this Dr Glue has done? You see we have a duty to protect private information given to us. It's netiquette."

"I'm sorry, Mr Lloyd. I can't divulge any details on this case except to say we wish to speak to this Dr Glue concerning a serious matter." The team had been ordered in no uncertain terms that news of the vandalism spree was not to leak out. The PCs and maintenance men who attended the scenes of the wrecked Gatsos had been warned. So far, so good. No member of the Press was aware of the case.

DC Smith knew she was on thin ground, and added: "Please let me assure you Mr Lloyd. Any information you can give me will be treated in the strictest confidence."

She was much more conciliatory than yesterday, thought Gavin.

"Well, I'm afraid I can't help you unless you do give me good reason. I spoke to one of our legal assistants last night and was informed what I basically already knew: you would need warrants to gain access to any SCATE information. But as I have said, SCATE is a law-abiding organisation. We are most certainly not anti-police. In fact, we want our police back on the roads instead of speed cameras. In fact, we have many police supporters. In fact, we have backing from high political contacts..."

DC Smith interrupted Gavin's party-spiel. "Listen, Mr Lloyd. I can easily arrange for some local officers to visit you and take you in for questioning if necessary. And, yes, warrants if you persist in obstructing the police in doing its duty."

She took a deep breath before adding: "If you wish me to believe SCATE is law-abiding, then you will help us. Trust me, all I can tell you is Dr Glue is wanted in connection with malicious damage to expensive road traffic equipment. I am sure you know what I am talking about. Now, this must go no further. No further, OK?"

DC Smith managed not to add: "Or else!"

So it was exactly what Gavin and Sue had anticipated; no more exotic a crime.

Sue got Gavin's attention by waving a piece of paper at him and mouthing that he should tell the copper about the profile.

"Fair enough, officer Smith. We are on the side of the police. But there isn't much I can tell you."

He gave DC Smith Dr Glue's profile.

"Is that it? Are you taking the piss?" the conciliatory copper was gone for the day. "What crap is that?"

Gavin tried his best to explain. He even added, just in case DC Smith didn't get it, that the email address would prove little use, as it was common practice for those seeking ultra-anonymity to employ many email addresses for a variety of reasons, generally dodgy. And few hosts checked your personal details when signing up for their accounts.

"I am NOT stupid, Mr Lloyd. Being a humble detective constable I merely hoped that an organisation like SCATE would be, well, a little more bloody ORGANISED. But you're telling me any old Mickey Mouse can post any old crap on your site and even you don't have a damned clue who he or she is?"

"Exactly. A bit like the police or like Crimewatch, accepting information from anonymous sources."

"It's nothing of the kind, Mr Lloyd. Thanks for your help, I suppose.

I'll be in touch."

"Frosty, indeed," said Sue, her eyes wide. "Suppose I can see her point, judging by what you had to give her."

"Suppose so," said Gavin. "At least we know they're just looking for another vandal. Wonder how they got hold of the name Dr Glue?"

"This looks like a job for Larry. Bet he'd find out in next to no time."

Gavin thought of the ace reporter with the Evening Standard. He'd spoken with Gavin several times while researching a news feature on speed cameras in the capital. Larry Evans was a mine of information, sources and resources.

"I didn't actually promise anything, but I think it was kind of implicit that I would keep her comments confidential."

"But little ol' me didn't promise anything," said Sue.

That day and the next passed with no further acerbic exchanges with DC Smith.

The weekend came and time for Gavin to quickly deal with those non-essential emails before tackling The Telegraph crossword. Saturday's was his favourite. This was his Saturday morning routine: answering as politely as possible a few general enquiries from worried, erring motorists. It usually sufficed to point them in the direction of the 'legal info' section on the website.

This morning his eye immediately veered to a note from the Humphrey Bellow. He opened the email and read:

You may be interested to tune into our leader's speech
from the conference today.
Regards, HB

Gavin checked the Conservative Party website and learned that the party was holding a mini-conference in Harrogate – one of those occasional rallying calls to the faithful. Samuel Owens was slated to deliver

SCATE

a keynote speech at 3pm.

"Stupid bloody time," thought Gavin. "I'll tape it."

He was booked for the day. His SCATE duties would be finished within the hour, he was on taxi duty for Kate, had promised to 'try better than last time, eh dad?' against Jim at snooker (he had no love for the game) and then he planned to watch the England-Scotland Rugby Union game down at the 'Dog'. A movie with Jim would close another fun-packed Saturday at the Lloyd household; Gavin would try and stay awake through it.

The day was going to schedule – almost. Gavin was walking home from the pub arm-in-arm with Sue. She had interrupted his viewing of a rare England Calcutta Cup defeat with 'exciting news.' They had seen the closing minutes of the game, supped up and were heading home to watch Gavin's tape of the Tory conference.

Samuel Owens was BRILLIANT, Sue had informed Gavin at the pub. She had been listening to the radio while doing some chores in her kitchen and, unaware of Gavin's email from Humphrey Bellow, had been thrilled by Owens's address to his members.

"I won't ruin it for you, but you just HAVE to hear it," she said.

Gavin fast-forwarded the tape to Owens's entrance on the podium as Sue made coffee.

They settled down to watch the Tory leader launch into a well-prepared tirade against the Government's transport policy.

He was scathing about their lack of investment in the railway infrastructure; their road policy was shambles. Was the audience aware that seven keenly-awaited by-passes were a total of 27 months behind schedule?

"So how does the Government treat those motorists fortunate enough not to be stuck in traffic jams in and around our major towns and cities? They increase the road fund tax, increase petrol duty, and, most damning of all, they embark with an evangelical zeal on yet another gimmick to fleece the poor motorist: speed cameras.

"Of course the secretary of state for transport would have us believe this new initiative – their 35th new initiative this term, in case anyone has lost count – is designed to improve road safety.

"Total rot! Road fatalities are increasing and more people are being seriously injured on our roads. The Government's response is this new *initiative*." Owens packed considerable venom into his delivery of 'initiative.' He had told Gavin of his intense dislike for the 'Government Of Gimmicks,' as he branded Britain's socialist rulers.

"Speed cameras – or safety cameras, as the secretary of state for transport would have us call them – are spearheading the Government's attempt to make our roads safer.

"Do these safety cameras trap the drunk-drivers who weekly maim and kill fellow motorists and pedestrians? Do these safety cameras nail the feckless or the reckless who motor around with absolutely no regard for their fellow citizens? Do these safety cameras catch people driving defective vehicles? No, no, no, my friends, they do not.

"They are excellent at catching motorists who speed, however. The good people at SCATE will tell you that. In case you aren't aware of SCATE, it is a small organisation aimed at restoring SENSIBLE policing to our roads instead of seeing motorists hounded and hammered in the pocket by these inhuman cash machines.

"I met the SCATE chairman only last week. He told me a story. This story concerned a 28-year-old Hertfordshire plumber with an impeccable driving record. Brian Simpson was caught by one of these safety cameras while travelling at 48 miles per hour in a 40 miles per hour zone. Silly Mr Simpson was fined £60 and had his licence endorsed for his crime. He did, however, manage to get his wife, Janice, to the hospital six minutes before she gave birth.

"I am delighted to inform the conference that mum and 6lb 7oz Lucy-Jane are doing fine."

Gavin beamed at his TV screen. He had to hand it to Samuel Owens, his researchers had done a splendid job in fleshing out Gavin's story. Gavin had had no idea of the guy's name or personal details.

"So, I ask the Prime Minister and his secretary of state for transport, do they truly feel our roads are safer for trapping the likes of Mr and Mrs Simpson?

"Surely a traffic policeman would have *assisted* the Simpsons in getting as quickly and as carefully to hospital rather than handing a worried father-to-be a speeding ticket.

"Sensible policing – that is what this country is crying out for. Not gimmicks. And I pledge the next Conservative Government to restoring sensible policing. To our streets and to our roads."

Owens closed with remarks about funding which drifted over Gavin's head.

"The good people at SCATE," Sue whistled. "I can see our chairman turning over a new political leaf."

"He's a class act, I'll say that for him," said Gavin. "And he did seem a decent bloke, too."

"Fancy popping over for a bite to eat later?" Sue asked.

"Thanks for the offer," said Gavin. "But I am tired and I did promise Jim I'd watch sequel number four of some adventure tosh. How about lunch tomorrow? Kate has a lift home."

"Can't, I already have a lunch date." There was mischief in her eyes.

"Oh. May I ask who?"

"Larry Evans. Don't worry, I'll be discreet."

Evans spotted Sue as she entered The Limetree, left his spot by the bar and gave her a friendly greeting: "How is my mystery woman? Hungry, I hope."

Sue had never met the Evening Standard man alone before. They had exchanged a few words when she accompanied Gavin for an interview at The Limetree. He had seemed friendly, intelligent, witty and trustworthy.

She had phoned his office to say she had some news he may be interested in, though really she was after his help. "It's not really a London story and it might not amount to much. Bit of a mystery really." Evans had been about to dash out to meet a contact and suggested lunch then – The Limetree just outside Romford.

Great food close to his home, on expenses - of course - even if the story didn't make it, and it always looked good with his news editor to be beavering away on a day off.

"Thanks for meeting me on a Sunday," said Sue.

"No, thank YOU, Sue. Got me out of a trek to Lakeside with the bride. Shopping should not be permitted on Sundays. Let's eat first, shall we? Food before business."

Sue was amazed at how briskly the 33-year-old skinny hack devoured a huge roast dinner.

"Ahhh, delicious. Won't find a better roast within 20 miles; and I'm an expert. What's it all about then? Sorry I was rushed when you called."

Sue told him the scant details after emphasising the absolute importance of keeping any mention of SCATE out of it. He almost felt like she wanted him to swear on a Bible at one point.

When she had finished, Evans looked at her quizzically. "Basically, Sue, we're talking about just another crackpot who smashed up a Gatso, right? Not some dastardly plot to topple the Government. I don't get it. What's the big deal?"

Inwardly, Sue was cut by the reporter's offhandedness. But she pressed on:

"But don't you see? I mean why would a detective phone us to help catch your common-and-garden lout? And, Larry, you really should have heard the woman copper on the phone to Gavin; didn't sound like she enjoyed helping old dears cross roads. She wouldn't tell him anything at first. Why not? As you say, what's the big deal if it IS just a crackpot? And how did she know this crackpot was called Dr Glue? And how did she know this crackpot used the SCATE forums? I know it may be nothing, Larry. But I was wondering if maybe you knew a reporter up north who may be interested?"

Got to give her ten out of ten for fervour, thought Evans.

"Fair point, Sue. A vandal with a handle might make a decent local story. I have a few contacts in Lancashire; best bet may be Owen Williams on the Evening Telegraph. I'll give him a buzz tomorrow."

He smiled at Sue, a little too indulgently for her liking.

Owen Williams was ten years older than Evans. They shared a healthy appetite for food and news, though Williams weighed in at least four stones heavier than his London counterpart. How did Larry stay so skinny?

Williams was most definitely interested in the story – or the few details gleaned from his chat with Evans – as speed cameras were big news to the locals and, more importantly, his editor. The editor's wife counted herself among the many thousands caught on camera. Silly cow had been doing 90-plus and deserved all she got, thought Williams.

No, the cops hadn't revealed anything about vandalism to the Press boys recently, he told Evans. And, no, he had never heard of a Dr Glue.

"Thanks for the call, chum. Won't mention your name, of course. I'll let you know how I get on."

Lancashire Constabulary's media office had nothing for Williams when he rang them on Tuesday morning. But, naturally, they would look into it and get back in touch. They were genuinely helpful most of the time – the relationship worked for both parties.

The return call came more quickly than Williams had expected; and not from the media folk but from DS Abrahams. He was cheeriness personified.

As anticipated, the team chasing Dr Glue had been whittled down. Many fingers were crossed, from the Chief Constable downwards, that this had been a one-off incident.

None of the forces involved had made any breakthrough. DC Smith had informed Abrahams of her conversation with Gavin Lloyd. She had conferred with the IT Department who suggested Lloyd was probably being straight with her. Still, they promised to have a scout around the Internet and scate.co.uk to see if they could pick up anything useful. They didn't, but they did waste a few police man-hours by chuckling at the forum posts.

"Hi Owen. Got a call from the media office. What's all this about, then? You free for a pint in an hour? How about the Vic?"

The Victoria And Albert was ten minutes' walk from the Evening Telegraph's offices in Blackburn.

It was packed with businessmen and women chatting away about everything under the sun. Lunchtime was always the same. Williams and Abrahams managed to find a relatively-quiet table and over two pints and a shared plate of ham and cheese sandwiches the detective sergeant told the reporter what he knew about the speed camera vandalism – or what he had only just cleared with Superintendent Charleston. Both agreed it was pointless trying to deny the story, for the sake of their good relationship with the local Press if nothing else.

Naturally, Williams could not reveal the source of his information. And he was careful to avoid mention of any Dr Glue. So was DS Abrahams as he ran through the nine areas vandalised.

SCATE

"That's about it, Owen. Can't give you much else, I'm afraid. You know the score, the chief's always worried about copycats. You can imagine he's raging about it. We didn't tell you earlier as all the forces involved agreed to keep it under wraps."

"Any idea who did it? You reckon just one guy working alone? Covered a lot of ground, didn't he?"

"Yes he did. We are following a few lines of enquiry and are hopeful."

"Oh VERY convincing, Colin! Come on, between you and me..."

"Listen, Owen. As soon as I have any more information you'll be the first to know. For now, the chief would be grateful if you could stress the need to keep our safety cameras operative as they are a key component in limiting the number of fatalities on our roads. How about something along the lines of 'Police are making steady progress...?' I have to dash. See what you can do, and I promise you'll be the first to know. Cheers."

"Cheers, Colin. Stay in touch."

The story made the following day's front page, with a photo of one of the wrecked Gatsos. The editor wasn't exactly happy at the scant details Owen had been able to provide and told him to work on it. Still, it was a decent enough story on a local topic of considerable interest and opinion.

Williams had ignored the sergeant's advice on how to compose his story, instead preferring "Lancashire Police are spearheading the hunt for a vandal who knocked out NINE speed cameras in ONE night."

A few hours after the paper hit the streets, Williams let a few contacts around the regions know of his scoop and suggested they may wish to follow it up with their local police forces.

By the following morning a Manchester freelance agency was letting the national newspapers know of the story "May make a few pars in your northern editions, lads?"

The Sun on Friday sent shockwaves through several northern forces.

GATSO'D!

Police launch massive hunt for Dr Glue

An unnamed source – no doubt for a couple of hundred quid – had told Britain's biggest-selling tabloid details of the wrecking-spree. Dr Glue was out in the open. The editor warmed to the story; a latter-day Dick Turpin. Plus it got the Royals off the front page.

As so often before, the paper's timing was immaculate.

Unaware that he was front-page news, Dr Glue had been plotting a weekend blitz – starting that very night.

CHAPTER FIVE

Taunted House

Sean Chapman was transport secretary in a Government constantly alert to any story with a political slant, especially one that appeared in The Sun. Chapman launched a probe into the northern vandalism as soon as he reached his desk.

A junior minister revealed he had received a routine note about the damage but was assured by police chiefs that it was most likely an isolated incident.

Within a few hours, the red-faced junior reported back to Chapman that the police chiefs had given him unfounded assurances based more on hope and that more vandalism had occurred that night.

"Where? How bad? Who? Have they caught him?" Chapman bombarded his colleagues with questions. Speed cameras were his 'initiative' and heaven help any employee who branded the scheme a gimmick in his presence.

"Same as before, I'm sad to report," replied Adam Scholes. "Perhaps even more widespread, and police believe this Dr Glue is behind it again. Several forces are sharing information and I've asked them to keep us informed."

"Thanks, Adam. Please make sure that they do. Owens and Mitchell are going to have a field day."

Samuel Owens and his shadow transport secretary Caroline Mitchell were naturally aware of The Sun story and were deciding how to respond - a tricky situation as they could hardly side with a criminal.

Mitchell was pleased with the question she intended to ask later that day in the House Of Commons: Mindless vandalism was the scourge of modern-day Britain, yet shouldn't this Government be asking itself just why the attacks on these detested speed cameras were steadily increasing?

By the time she stood up to speak the situation had developed into more than a steady increase.

Earlier that morning, Superintendent Charleston and DS Abrahams were discussing whether any of their officers could have leaked the details of Dr Glue to The Sun when Charleston was called away to take a call from a colleague in Reading.

He returned with a grave face to inform Abrahams: "He's been at it again. Down south this time."

"That was Alan Carter from Berkshire. His boys have dealt with three vandalised Gatsos this morning. They have information coming in from neighbouring forces, too. Dr Glue left his calling card again."

"Shit!" said Abrahams, smacking his fist into the palm of his hand. "You reckon we're looking at another nine-timer?"

Det Supt Charleston didn't dare guess. "I'd better warn the chief. You take charge of liaising with the other forces. Make sure we get everything they've got. Oh, and make a few discreet inquiries to see if any of our mob tipped off that bloody tabloid rag."

News of Dr Glue's exploits filtered into several police force HQs throughout the day and loaded onto the national police database. The doctor had been busy – 12 strikes in a night.

From roughly 10pm to 3am Dr Glue had vandalised speed cameras from the M25, along the M4 and up the M5, just south of Birmingham. Once again he had taken minor detours. He clearly knew where to look for his targets.

The same *modus operandi* – though he seemed to have run out of plastic plates on the home run as the last two had parts of blown-out tyres well-glued inside the cameras; with the business card.

More man-hours and considerable cost was deployed replacing the Gatsos. Officers read the scant details from the files; they quizzed their northern colleagues; and they scratched their heads.

There was little point in attempting to conceal the news from the Press. The hounds had scented a good story and were in pursuit.

The Government went on the offensive on TV, radio and in the Commons: this reckless lout was risking lives, not simply damaging valuable safety equipment. Caroline Mitchell deftly negotiated her way around the vandalism issue and appeared to have won the day by a narrow margin. Speed cameras became the hot new topic. By the time the Saturday morning papers had finished, Dr Glue was viewed as either a total degenerate lacking respect for the law of the land or a lovable rogue who was giving the Government's road traffic policy a kick where it hurts.

The papers were split. So it appeared was the country. Many knew someone who had been caught on one, celebrities revealed to the Press they had been unfortunate, too, footballers just having the edge over TV soap stars.

Gavin Lloyd helped The Sunday Times hastily put together a special feature for that weekend's paper. The country got to hear of Dr Glue's posts at the SCATE forums. He'd been back there on Saturday lunchtime and his post made The Sunday Times' front page:

**Dr Glue
Who Are You?
Poor, Old Cops
Don't Have a Clue**

He was now out in the open and teasing his pursuers. The SCATE website was overloaded and spent 90 minutes offline late Sunday afternoon. News and motoring sites had made links to scate.co.uk to help readers find out more on Britain's Number One vandal.

New sign-ups to the forums topped the thousand-mark at 7.10pm that day. The most popular topic thread was started by Osama Bin Speedin and headed 'Friends Of Dr Glue'. The rants flowed in from people relating their sorry tales.

Gavin made the disclaimer more prominent, for his own peace of mind and to spare any embarrassment to organisations that supported his cause: *SCATE did not condone speeding and was most definitely against vandalism of any kind.*

Gavin also had a busy day fielding media questions. No, like the cops, Gavin didn't have a clue who Dr Glue was. A round of phone calls over the weekend confirmed neither did any of his SCATE friends.

At the end of a long day, he and Sue Jenkins sat down for a tot of Frank McIvor's finest.

"What a bloody day," sighed Gavin.

"The people just love a good mystery – a real life one is even better. Wait till the morning: people will be shopping neighbours and workmates up and down the country. Wonder if any of the papers will offer a reward?"

"Ha! The smart money says The Sun will. Be nice if we could find him first. I'm really not comfortable with him, Sue. I don't want the site turning into a forum for yobs to unite and plot trouble. Think of all the work we've put in."

"I know. How many posts did you have to delete?"

"Well, just three or four myself. The software automatically blocked those with foul language. I feel the need to redress the balance and was wondering about asking a cop to give the police view."

"Or maybe our pals in Government?" Sue smiled.

"Not as daft as it sounds, Sue. Yes. Maybe try that. Looks like a manic Monday approaching. I also may try ringing round some others to check if they know the doctor. I ran a trace on the IP addresses he posts from. None are the same; so I would guess he is logging on from Internet cafes. Clever sod."

"Who you going to call? I can only think of one bloke who may be able to help: Pete Hampson."

"Snap!"

"But he's inside."

"Yes, out west somewhere. I have a letter from him. Never been inside a prison. I'll see how one goes about visiting jailbirds."

Pete Hampson was a guest of Her Majesty at Shepton Mallet in Somerset. He was seven weeks into a six-month sentence for torching a Gatso. He'd been arrested by an off-duty police officer.

Hampson was the man behind the 'John' voice that phoned Gavin after reading his letter all those months ago.

The meeting Hampson had arranged in a west London pub was a shambles. A motley group of people Hampson had contacted sat around a table in a hired room and let off steam against speed cameras. There was no agenda and people gradually drifted away to attend more pressing matters with a vague promise to meet again. There would be no second meeting, and, in fact, one of the group was arrested for drink-driving on his way home.

Gavin and Hampson, though, stuck around and talked until closing time.

The softly-spoken Welshman sold novelty items to the retail trade and made regular trips to the south-east.

He worked long hours for little reward but managed to keep his head above water. He was thoroughly pissed off, he told Gavin, at being done for carefully driving his Cavalier just seven miles over the limit near Brighton.

He was returning from handing over £200 of cheap jewellery to a trader on the pier.

"Just forty quid profit in that for me, not counting my petrol. Forty quid! And then I get hit with a bloody sixty quid fine. Why work your balls off, eh?"

It was clear that 33-year-old Hampson didn't have much idea of where his protest was leading him. But he was angry enough to want to do something. Gavin was the more organised of the pair. Though Hampson never got round to joining in the SCATE group discussions, he had met the others on a trip to Great Wilton, and he kept in touch with Gavin via email and the occasional phone call. He encouraged a few friends in Wales to join the forums and their informal group did manage to have a few angry letters published in regional papers.

There was always an edge to Hampson, however. "Something dodgy about people in that line of business," said Sue Jenkins.

A few posts in Welsh from one of his gang had had to be deleted. An online translation tool had shown that they had been promoting vandalism against cameras.

Hampson went over the edge one Friday night in Cardiff. He was fuming after being landed with another sixty bloody quid fine. It had been a bad day at the office; he went out drinking and took out a petrol can when he arrived home.

He walked a couple of hundred yards to a nearby Gatso and had himself a bonfire. He was watching the blaze from a dozen yards away, petrol can in hand, when the police constable arrested him. At least he hadn't been driving.

He had written to Gavin from the prison, a quite tearful note apologising for letting his good friend down.

Yes, Gavin would try and see Pete Hampson; even if it proved fruitless in his search for information on Dr Glue, it would be decent to check on his one-time acquaintance's welfare.

He was about to phone the prison when he got a call from DC Smith.

"Hello Mr Lloyd. DC Smith here. We're sending some local police officers to see you this afternoon. I do hope that is convenient."

A statement rather than a question.

"I have told them you are willing to co-operate in our enquiries. Is that still the case or will they need warrants? It would look bad for SCATE if word got out that you refused to help the police. I mean your new Tory friends would drop you like a hot brick."

Gavin disliked the woman more deeply every time he spoke with her. But he maintained his composure.

"Of course, DC Smith. Naturally we wish to help. As I have told you before, we are not anti-police; far from it. I wish you had told me more information earlier. I certainly didn't mean to appear unhelpful."

"Smooth bastard," thought DC Smith but she told Gavin: "Thank you. Two officers will arrive at 2.30pm. They will require access to your computer files. Please do not attempt to remove any items in the meantime. Goodbye."

Gavin had no need to wipe anything. That had been done, not that there was much to be worried about, anyway.

He and Sue had decided to raise the police issue with the other SCATE members and all had agreed, on legal advice, to assist the police whenever they asked for their help.

The police had a lawful right to examine their files if they were investigating criminal activity, but the files could not be kept on any police database.

Most of the scate.co.uk information was in the public domain; all Gavin would be able to show the police was a few private email addresses – probably fictitious.

Gavin made enquiries with Shepton Mallet prison, booked a visit for that Thursday and read through the morning papers while waiting for his police visitors. He smiled as he read. True to form The Sun had come up with a reward – a spanking brand new £25,000 Subaru Impreza (as favoured by our traffic police, if you can ever find one) for information on the identity of Dr Glue.

The Government and the police had been as busy as the media men that weekend. The officers soon to visit Gavin were part of a taskforce established on the Sunday. The Safety Cameras Taskforce was headed by Alison Hayes, assistant chief constable of Essex. Its headquarters were in Harlow, scene of the infamous Lloyd trial. The SCT had a base group of eight officers under ACC Hayes, plus liaison officers with each force. Lancashire police provided two officers: DS Abrahams and DC Smith.

The taskforce was entrusted with the apprehension of vandals and the prevention of further outbreaks.

ACC Hayes was to act as the chief police spokesman on safety cameras. She had direct access to transport secretary Sean Chapman. She fully intended to kick-start this avenue to promotion by nailing Dr Glue. She had wasted no time that weekend, ensuring all the communication channels and data collection procedures met her satisfaction. By the time she was driven to her Southend home late on Sunday night she was content that Dr Glue would be found within 48 hours. That Lancashire lassie may prove their best route for starters. So DC Smith had made her call to Gavin.

"Good afternoon, Mr Lloyd is it? We're from the SCT."

"Hello. Yes, I'm Gavin Lloyd. I'm from SCATE," he quipped. "Just been hearing about the SCT on the radio. How can I help? Fancy a cup of coffee? Or tea?"

He was going to be as co-operative as possible he told DS Wickford and DS Pierce as he prepared two impossibly-sugary mugs of coffee.

DS Wickford was there to question Gavin, DS Pierce to examine any SCATE computers. They were under instructions to tread lightly as there was no evidence linking SCATE with any criminal activity. But ACC Hayes had added that if he was unhelpful they should bring Lloyd in for further questioning and she would arrange warrants for the requisition of his computers.

There would be no need for that; Gavin was on his best behaviour, even if he wasn't quite as sugary as the coffee the two cops consumed by the gallon.

Gavin told DS Pierce he had backed up all the information so the officer was free to roam around the voluminous files and folders on his SCATE PC on a "read-only basis".

DS Stuart Pierce, a 28-year-old from Harlow, knew his way around the intricacies of most computer systems. He had joined the police after becoming hooked on forensics during his student days in Manchester. He had graduated with a second-class honours degree in computer technology. Part of his studies had involved watching police trap an Internet group who peddled child-pornography.

Computers were more of a hobby for him these days, but he was an ideal addition to the SCT. He could call on the IT department if he felt he was being hoodwinked.

He settled down to examine the SCATE files as Gavin and DS Wickford remained in the kitchen for "a little chat."

DS Steve Wickford had no need to grill Gavin, nor apply the thumbscrews. The two men got on rather well. The questioning was gentle and Gavin was more than happy to take DS Wickford through his personal agonies at the hands of speed cameras – Gavin was delighted to hear the copper refer to them as *speed* cameras rather than *safety* cameras.

He showed him the letter that he had mailed a year ago, he told him how he launched SCATE and gave him details on the other SCATE members – all fine people, he assured the sergeant.

"And all have alibis for the nights Dr Glue was doing his dirty work?" probed DS Wickford with a slight laugh.

"Oh, I am sure they do," replied Gavin in equal measure.

DS Wickford was the same age as Gavin; a couple of inches taller. Chelmsford was his base station. He had a friendly demeanour. He didn't strike Gavin as a cop to clean up the Essex badlands.

Gavin was wrong. DS Wickford could be as tough as any TV hard man detective when the situation required it. He had helped put away some real nasty villains: drug dealers, rapists, gangland mobsters, even a noted hitman responsible for at least three hits that the police had been able to pin on him.

Now he was chasing a vandal. True, this guy was a serial vandal who was costing the police a great deal of time and money but he was still way down DS Wickford's list of public enemies. He was intelligent enough not to share his private thoughts with ACC Hayes.

He kept them from Gavin, too, as he asked him one more time:

"OK then Mr Lloyd, just so I can inform my boss, you have no idea who this Dr Glue is? And as far as you are aware nor do any of your members?"

"That's right officer. We have been wracking our brains to come up with the name of anyone we have been in contact with who could be responsible. Not a clue. Sorry."

"I believe you, mate. Really I do. If you do hear of anything – ANY-THING – which could be useful to us give me a ring on this number."

He handed Gavin a card and shouted through to his colleague: "You almost finished, Stu?"

"Give me a few more minutes. Maybe you and Mr Lloyd can come through here and see just what information I am taking."

The two sergeants teased Gavin by claiming to be the friendliest coppers on the SCT. They were grateful for his co-operation, and for all the coffee. They wanted him to know they trusted him, and he could trust them.

DS Pierce informed Gavin about the attempts the previous day by the IT department to trace Dr Glue via the IPs. Like Gavin they had reached the conclusion he wasn't using his own computer but posting from public computers, maybe in cafes, libraries, airports or schools.

He told Gavin he was taking information on 12 people in his personal address book.

Could Gavin kindly confirm the details on these people were accurate and up to date? They were, as far as Gavin knew.

The friendliest coppers on the SCT said their farewells, emphasising once again just how grateful they would be if Gavin got in touch with any useful information.

"Find anything useful?" DS Wickford asked his colleague as they drove back to their Harlow HQ.

"Naah. Just got those addresses for a few routine checks tomorrow. You have any joy?"

"Nope. Not that I expected much. But he has given me a note for the chief."

"What note?"

"He wants a copper to write a piece for his bloody website. Thinks it would be wizardly timely if it came from our beloved Ms Hayes. He wants to show his happy band is peaceful and fair-minded."

"She'll love that! I'm so glad he gave it to you to hand over. You can tell her how we got on today while you're at it. Make you flavour of the month."

"What did the silly cow expect? I made a few quick calls this morning and the local boys told me our Gavin was squeaky clean. Well squeaky if you discount the speeding. Four times in six months the silly sod. Seems a nice silly sod, though."

Gavin had indeed been fair-minded with the cops, giving them everything they asked for and going out of his way to help. But he just happened to keep from them his intended visit to the nick holding Pete Hampson. Of course, he would pass on any valuable information.

ACC Hayes at present had little valuable information. She was disappointed when her sergeants relayed details of their visit to the SCATE organisation. The 43-year-old stocky spinster was convinced they held the key. Like DC Smith before her she was adamant they knew who this villain was?

She gave DS Wickford a more thorough grilling than Gavin Lloyd had received. She threw Lloyd's request for a website article to one side in contempt before checking herself and telling Wickford to get one of the traffic boys to write a piece. She would want to see it before it was passed on. And keep a close eye on these SCATE people. She briskly departed the room.

"Certainly, ma'am," DS Wickford said to her back.

The only other leads that day had come from the IT department who had managed to track down three of the computers Dr Glue had used to post his forum messages. Tomorrow officers were due to visit the Metropole Hotel at Birmingham's National Exhibition Centre complex, an Internet café in Kendal and Gatwick Airport. Kendal seemed their best hope of success. Who would be able to recall someone who used a computer at a major London airport or a large, busy hotel?

She worked late as usual before summoning her driver shortly after 8pm. "Watch out on the 127 – some new cameras there," she told George Ravelli, without humour.

They drove back to Southend in silence, ACC Hayes in the back with her eyes closed – thinking, not napping.

George always waited for her to wave him away before he would drive the two miles to his home in a slightly more modest part of the seaside resort.

He noticed her stop on the path leading to her front door. It was dark, too. George wound down his window. "Everything all right, ma'am?"

She waved him to join her. He did as bade and the senior police officer pointed at the security light which usually illuminated her path and a good section of her front lawn when anyone approached within 15 yards of the house. Something was blocking the light.

"Don't touch anything, George. Just come with me."

They edged towards her front door. No problems there. She could open the door. She switched on the hall light so they could have a clearer view of the outside light. There was a thin, reddish, round disc covering the light; a white substance oozing out of one side.

"Christ all-bloody-mighty!" exclaimed ACC Hayes to George's disgust.

An hour later George was on his way home, leaving behind two coppers with ACC Hayes. It took them 35 minutes of delicate chiselling to prise the plastic plate free more or less intact. The light came on immediately, temporarily blinding one of the cops.

"Looks like the same stuff, ma'am," said the other officer as he allowed ACC Hayes closer inspection of the offending object. "There's a card stuck inside."

He let ACC Hayes read it for herself: Glue Loves Ya Baby!

CHAPTER SIX

Spitting Image Of The PM

The Yamaha Muscle-XJR1300 was a powerful beast. Its rider was slight of frame, made to appear bulkier by the heavy leathers he sported. The rucksack on his back was half his size. But it weighed little this night; just one job was on the cards.

He parked by some trees in a half-full council car park just off a main road. He tied his cycle helmet to his rucksack and walked the quarter of a mile through the leafy, expensive suburb until he found the address he was seeking. He walked around for a few minutes.

The coast was clear. He threw his rucksack over the hedge and his body followed right behind it. He edged alongside the house wall, to avoid setting off the security light. He took out his tools. He smeared a layer of white glue over a red plastic plate – the kind used for picnics – and neatly arranged a white card in the centre. Quick as a flash he placed the plate over the security light and held it firm for five seconds. He left by the same route. He had been at work for less than 30 seconds. Shame the rate for the job wasn't much.

He felt rewarded, however, as he walked the opposite way around the block and back to his motorcycle. Within five minutes the Yamaha had left Southend and was purring back to Redditch, a growing Worcestershire town.

He arrived back at his one-bed roomed flat shortly after 10pm.

"She should be home by now," he smiled as he took off his helmet and then his curly wig. He scratched what little natural hair he had.

Dr Glue had a shower and then dashed out to grab a couple of pints before retiring for the night. He slept more soundly than ACC Hayes.

The garden at the home of Essex's most senior-ranking female officer resembled a major crime scene next day. Nosey neighbours managed to discover that poor Alison's property had been vandalised. No, the police could not tell them the nature of the attack.

John Jacobs already knew. He was in Southend bright and early to conclude a sale with a fellow scrap-dealer. Jimmy Mortimer just happened to be a drinking buddy of George Ravelli's, and AAC Hayes's driver had told Jimmy of the crime in hushed tones over a pint and a game of darts the previous night.

J.J. was mightily amused. He shook hands on the deal, went to his car and rang the SCATE-phone on his mobile. Sue Jenkins answered. She was always there these days, he thought.

Sue's guffaws did not become a lady. She thanked J.J. and looked forward to seeing him soon. She told Gavin and they agreed she should contact Larry Evans – the London reporter was angry with himself for missing out on the Dr Glue scoop which had landed in his lap.

Evans was delighted and thanked Sue profusely but had to rush to check it out. Hopefully it would make that day's later editions.

Evans contacted the taskforce HQ immediately. The police were wise enough not to lie to the Press on issues involving their own – unless they felt they really had to, of course.

Their refusal to either confirm or deny the story was good enough for Evans.

Evans informed his editor who told his reporter to bash out 300 words ASAP while he cleared the front page.

With the help of a fellow reporter who checked some biographical details on Hayes and fished out some background on Dr Glue's attacks, Evans had the story ready inside 20 minutes. The Chief

Sub-Editor swung into action and within the hour the 'slip' edition was rolling off the presses:

DR GLUE HITS TOP ESSEX COP

"Makes sure it gets as deep into Essex as possible," the editor told the circulation and distribution departments. "Especially around Southend. And make sure there are plenty of bills up." He loved the buzz of a good, late story; much more if it involved some bigwig on his patch. And Alison Hayes was edging higher up the bigwig league since assuming her role with the SCT.

"Well done, Larry."

Evans felt pleased. Fortunately, his editor wasn't aware that his reporter had missed the original Dr Glue story – not that it was a good London story at that stage.

He would have liked more facts and a police reaction but he was thankful for small mercies – the scoop was his; the morning papers could chase up the details. None of them would get the details of Dr Glue's calling card, however. If that leaked out heads would roll, ACC Hayes had warned.

Many senior police officers have just two moods: grumpy and raging. Alison Hayes was not feeling grumpy when she was shown the front page of the Evening Standard. The distribution team had done their editor proud and managed to hit Essex. The thoughtful DS Wickford had bought a copy after spotting a billboard. He had been brave enough to take it to the ACC.

DS Wickford had to give the girl credit; after her rage had quelled she was more concerned with how the taskforce was progressing that day than how news of her embarrassment had leaked out. Professional to the core; she wanted a result above all else.

The visits to Birmingham and Gatwick had not surprisingly proved useless. "Still waiting to hear from the Lankies on Kendal, ma'am."

DS Abrahams and DC Smith were returning back to Blackburn at that very moment. The M6 was a pain at that hour.

They had had an enlightening afternoon, even if they would not be able to report much significant progress to the Harlow HQ.

Colin Abrahams was 36 years old and felt slightly uncomfortable having to play second fiddle to a woman nine years his junior as they entered the Lakeland Internet Café.

She was the computer geek and would be doing most of the talking.

The Lakeland Internet Café was run by a polite, mid-20s Asian man who, once he had recovered from his initial shock at a police visit, was more than happy to talk them through his business.

The premises were bigger than the police officers had expected, double-fronted on a busy main street in the centre of town.

It sold hot and cold drinks and served an assortment of cold snacks.

A few locals regularly came in to log onto one of the 20 computers – lunchtime and early evening were his busiest periods. But most of his trade came from casuals – visitors to the Lake District town who wanted to send a few emails to friends.

Sorry, he couldn't help them on Dr Glue. No-one stood out on the time they mentioned. The owner, however, was able to point out a table holding four computers. "Judging by the IP addresses and the time you say he posted this message it would probably have been one of those four."

It was a busy business; most people came and paid for 30 minutes or an hour online. Some would not use half their time. Always people coming and going, he told them. But certainly he would keep an eye out for anyone suspicious.

"Thanks for that, Helen. I felt a bit useless in there," DS Abrahams said as he drove back to the station.

"No probs, Guv. Let's hope our doctor does pass through the quaint Lakeland Internet Café again. Still, I can't see our new friend being able to clock many customers – not if he's running a one-man show and is open every hour God sends. Don't we have a law against that kind of thing?"

DS Abrahams chuckled: "He'll be rich and retired long before us."

DC Smith stood over the sergeant as he wrote out the brief report to send to Harlow, with a copy to Superintendent Charleston.

The 27-year-old's green eyes twinkled as she guided her boss through a few technical details he had struggled to digest. DS Abrahams was gradually becoming more *au fait* with the Internet and computers and all that junk, but he readily admitted it wasn't his cup of tea.

Together they browsed through that day's reports from officers across the land. No-one had much to report. Both gasped as they read the details of Dr Glue's raid on the home of ACC Hayes. They shivered in mock horror as they saw the red warning sign about divulging information to outside parties. They knew of Alison Hayes's reputation if not the lady in person.

DC Abrahams was about to log-off when an update popped into the system: a file from Transport Secretary Sean Chapman. "Let's have a quick look at this," he told his constable.

When he tried to open the folder his computer asked him for a password.

"Strange," the two officers muttered in harmony.

They tried twice more before deciding to pack up for the day. They had a quick drink at the 'police pub' round the corner where fellow officers were keen to learn how the hunt for Public Vandal Number One was progressing.

Then they retired to their respective homes for the evening: Abrahams to his 1930s semi for a night in front of the TV with his wife and three kids; Smith to her smart new flat in an upmarket development which was barely within reach of a copper's salary – if you were content with just the one room, that is.

She dined quickly, then passed two hours surfing the Internet. She browsed through scate.co.uk while waiting for her Shania Twain MP3s to download. A strange mix, but Helen Smith was hooked on both.

Two hundred and fifty miles away in Harlow, AAC Hayes was still in her music-free office reading for a second time the files from Sean Chapman; password-protected as they were for the ACC's eyes only.

A personal note from Chapman expressed his distress at hearing of the attack on her home and he insisted she take adequate measures to protect herself and any other officers she felt were potential targets.

The other files were cost assessments, recommended solutions, Government aims, media releases, and, finally, a report on the success or otherwise of camera experiments from a few carefully selected foreign countries.

The government, it seemed, was going on the offensive. Though there was grim reading amidst the dogma.

The spate of attacks by Dr Glue had caused irreparable damage to 16 safety cameras. These had been replaced at a cost of approximately £42,500 each (costs varied, according to ease of access). Others were being repaired, though the costs would be considerable.

The company that supplied the cameras to most parts of the UK deserved praise for the efficiency and speed with which they reacted to this problem.

However, the costs of missed fines were estimated to be in the region of £3.5m.

That figure brought a whistle from the lips of ACC Hayes. It made a minor dent in the £160m revenue the treasury and the police shared from speeding fines annually.

Isolated acts of vandalism occurred elsewhere. True, they were a nuisance, but primarily the acts of cretins who were being dealt with by the law.

One of the files revealed that the transport department had written to judges requesting that they deal with offenders to the maximum of their powers to ward off the copycats.

ACC Hayes read on. She was familiar with most of the facts. The Government's decision to raise speeding fines to £70 would be on the statute books in early May.

The Government was pressing ahead with a new initiative to force criminals to pay a fine supplement into a victims support fund.

The deployment of safety cameras and assorted technological equipment would continue as quickly as possible in order to release police officers for other duties.

Within 18 months the target was 10,000 cameras protecting the roads of Britain.

Following the comments of some senior police chiefs, the Government was re-assessing its mandate that cameras should be restricted to accident blackspots.

There was a morass of facts, figures and advice – what to say and what not to say in public or to the Press – and there was one file which made ACC Hayes feel uncomfortable.

The Safety Cameras Taskforce had been established to ensure the safety cameras programme went ahead as planned and on schedule. It had wide-ranging powers to draft in help from any of Britain's police forces and was charged with the apprehension and conviction of the gang responsible for many recent attacks.

What bloody gang? thought Hayes. It was just the work of one man; well two men at most, she had convinced herself.

There were a few far from helpful suggestions from civil servants on how to assist the police. One ludicrous scheme was to have unmarked police cars patrolling the roads on the lookout for vandals.

Her thoughts were drifting when DS Pierce burst into her office. "Sorry to interrupt, ma'am. But I thought you'd want to hear this right away. The boys up in Northumberland are holding somebody – could be our man. Some info is coming through now. Want to have a look?"

"Great news. Thank you, Pierce. I'll be one minute. Oh, and please *do* knock in future."

"Yes. Sorry, ma'am. One other thing: it was in the Prime Minister's constituency."

Hexham is a quaint Northumberland town on the banks of the River Tyne and close to the border with Scotland. It boasts a National Hunt racecourse and a splendid abbey which has under-gone numerous changes in its 1400-year existence.

It was served at Westminster by the Right Honourable Laurence Carr – the leader of the Labour Party and Prime Minister for seven years. Prime Minister Carr was an outsider but had emerged as one of Hexham's favourite sons.

Ronald Forster was not ever likely to figure among Hexham's list of favourites – no matter how lengthy that list grew.

Ronnie was always in scrapes with the law; minor stuff such as drunk and disorderly, breaches of the peace, street scuffles.

One night, out of sheer boredom, he and his sidekick Brent Scowcroft had dreamed up a scheme. They 'borrowed' a mechanical digger and some heavy-duty tools from a nearby building site and went to work.

The Gatso they had part dug up, part cut down lay undisturbed in a little-used allotment, until they had a visit from Brent's cousin.

Ricky Munroe visited Brent now and then when life with his parents in the Durham village of Middleton-in-Teesdale became too demanding, which was usually when they nagged him to find work.

Ricky persuaded his hosts to put the Gatso to good use.

He had read about Dr Glue in the papers. Wouldn't it be a riot if they stuck the Prime Minister's mask on it and planted it in the town centre? There were no objections.

One bright March morning, the sight of a speed camera rooted in a garden bed outside the abbey greeted the gentle folk of Hexham as they scurried about their business. A Spitting Image-style latex mask of their beloved Prime Minister had been stretched over the head of the Gatso, making the caricature appear even more grotesque.

Police 'crime scene' tape circled the garden bed. Amused onlookers obeyed the tape boundaries until the police arrived and with extra manpower hauled the Gatso away.

The mask proved Ricky's undoing. It was a gift for his cousin, bought while waiting his bus in Barnard Castle. It had his fingerprints all over it. Within a couple of hours the police had a match and two detectives were waiting for the small-time villain when he arrived back at his parent's house that Tuesday afternoon.

Ricky Munroe was taken to Durham City police HQ rather than Northumberland.

Back in Harlow, the SCT team read two sets of reports. The Northumberland police sent details of the incident and, yes, super glue had been used to stick the mask firmly onto the Gatso. It would prove impossible to take off the mask without destroying it.

DS Wickford fired back some questions: could they have the glue checked out by their forensic people; was there a calling card?

Durham police were awaiting instructions before formally interviewing Munroe. They provided the SCT with his criminal record – two fines for petty theft and one for breach of the peace.

Another long day beckoned for ACC Hayes. Her demeanour changed from hopeful to despondent as news filtered back.

No calling card, common superglue – no joy at the Northumberland end.

An hour later the Durham detectives quizzing Munroe said he had confessed to doing it alone on the spur on the moment. They didn't believe him.

He claimed he owned no vehicle at present and had not done so for several months. Checks proved this was true. They also had discovered he had never been Gatso'd and had no convictions for any type of motoring offence.

He had given them alibis for times of the attacks in the south and on the ACC's home but couldn't recall where he was or what he was doing on February 26-27th. The detectives believed him but were having the alibis checked out.

"Just a bloody copycat," snapped ACC Hayes. "Where's George? Let's go home."

Northumberland police did manage to get Brent Scowcroft to own up to being involved in his cousin's prank. Scowcroft also took the rap for destroying the Gatso.

Ronnie Forster would be in his debt when he had served his six-month's time.

One lucky Hexham photographer made a killing selling a snap of the masked Gatso to the national, local and even international Press. The picture made the front pages in all the British daily papers.

He was kind enough to let Gavin Lloyd use it for free on the SCATE website.

Scate.co.uk was still steadily growing in popularity, but other sites were springing up. More militant message boards appeared; some were asking for legal sanctions, in Gavin's opinion.

He broke up his journey to Pete Hampson's prison by visiting a company which sold Internet servers. He arranged to lease his own server at a cut-price rate as long as he featured the company's advert prominently.

Hampson was one of 215 inmates at HMP Shepton Mallet – a former military base for British and American forces during the Second World War.

Inaccessible by public transport, Gavin was glad he was back behind the wheel as he drove the 40 miles from his hotel to the prison. He was allowed 30 minutes with the prisoner at 11am. The prison was less formidable a fortress than expected. The guards were polite and welcoming. Notices reminded guests of prohibited actions inside the visiting rooms.

Gavin told Hampson he looked in good health.

"Three square meals a day – some of 'em almost edible," he joked with his old friend. "It's not bad in here, to be honest. I'm learning my lesson and being looked after OK."

"Good. Thanks for writing, Pete. Sorry I haven't been in touch. Too busy to fart some days."

Pleasantries over, Hampson asked: "So what brings you all this way down here? Not just my health, I bet."

Gavin told Hampson about Dr Glue and his activities. Hampson had seen the papers. "We are allowed some small luxuries in here, you know. You're thinking he might be one of my old boyos?"

"Well you Welsh were always a fiery lot – no pun intended. I read a couple of others got caught following your example. Tut, tut."

"Yeah! Stupid bastards! At least Rhys seems to be heeding my very sound advice. I did worry about him. But this doctor seems much smarter than the crowd I hung around with. Gotta hand it to him. He's even made a few miserable buggers in here smile."

"Well I'd be grateful if you hear anything."

"Why yer you so interested? Fancy being a copper?"

"I'm really not sure, Pete. I guess it's just the police interest in us. I swear this woman cop from Lancashire is convinced it's one of us. I expect to see her tailing me on her broomstick one of these days."

"What would you do if you found out before the cops? Tell 'em?"

"I haven't really thought that through either, Pete."

"Listen, Gav, for old time's sake and for doing a great job, I'll see if I can find out anything from the old crowd. But Chris Jones is my only regular visitor. Just promise me one thing: you'll deal with the guy yourself and not hand him over to the cops. I'm sure we both agree with his sentiments if not his means. And heaven help me if anyone in here finds out I've helped the cops. I'm sure a friendly visit from Neil Proust could persuade Dr Glue that peaceful protest is the way forward. Deal?"

Gavin smiled as he considered Pete's offer. A visit from Neil Proust could probably persuade anyone of anything Neil wanted.

"Cheers Pete. Deal." And he offered his hand. "Glad we had this little chat. You've helped clear a few things in my mind. When you expect to be out?"

"Four weeks if I'm a good boy. Can't wait. Guess what I miss most?"

"Hmmm, probably not being able to cheer on a very mediocre Rugby Union team."

"Nope. We can watch that shower on TV. The boozer. Not just the beer, but the whole bloody idea of being free to go and join the boys for a few pints and talk gibberish till the cows come home."

"Well work up a thirst mate. Keep in touch either way, and let me know when you get out and I may even buy you a pint. Take care of yourself."

"You, too, Gav. Give my love to the crowd back home – even that bloody flash Essex geezer. Drive safely – and watch out for flashing lights."

Nine days later a letter arrived at the Lloyd household. It was from HMP Shepton Mallet. What a weird note. Pete had covered both sides of a single sheet of paper with ramblings. The paragraph indentation was bizarre, too. But the postscript alerted Gavin Lloyd.

Took your advice and decided to tackle The Telegraph crossword to pass the time. Too tricky for me, mate. Guess you need an eye for an acronym to solve that. Out in 17 days with a bit of luck. Don't forget that pint you owe me.'

What on earth was Pete on about? They'd never discussed crosswords. Gavin jumped up and grabbed a pen and a sheet of paper from a drawer. He flicked through the letter again and began jotting down the first letter of the 11 crisp paragraphs.

K-E-V-I-N-A-L-L-I-N-N.

Kevin Allinn. The name meant nothing to Gavin. He soon found it on the scate.co.uk database, though.

CHAPTER SEVEN

Frozen In The Headlights

While Gavin Lloyd was driving back from his prison visit, Kevin Allinn was sitting in front of his computer. He was checking the latest updates on the SCATE website's interactive map.

Scattered around his seat lay photographs and maps; road maps and ordnance survey maps. He couldn't make up his mind where to make his next strike. Scotland appealed to him but was a bloody long haul. So, was it to be South Yorkshire or East Anglia?

East Anglia won the game of roulette in his head. He could perhaps pay those nice people at SCATE a visit on his way home.

There was a race meeting at Newmarket the following day and there were two Gatsos close to the racetrack that he would like to have fun with.

He could annoy the police forces of three counties: Norfolk, Suffolk and Essex. It had the added blessing of being a compact route for his Yamaha at night.

Once his mind was made up, the 30-year-old courier neatly folded away the paperwork he would not be needing. An impressive 18-page dossier remained. It listed all the known Gatsos in the four counties; almost 1,500 potential targets.

All were colour-coded on Allinn's PC.

He had made a mental note to avoid the red ones since the news of his work had reached the national Press. Red signified the risky ones in high-visibility areas or with poor access for his motorbike. Yellow marked cameras on roads he was unfamiliar with. He decided those were a no-go tonight. From the blacks and greens he made a list of 30 possibles, some he had passed before, others were recently erected. Allinn worked out a looping route. He would start near Newmarket and swing round the coast of the region before arriving on the M11 close to Alison Hayes's SCT HQ in Harlow. Tempting though it was to pay the Harlow taskforce a home call he would make his way home via the M25 and M1.

While a couple of dozen cards slowly edged out of his Epson printer, Allinn checked his other supplies. Six plastic plates remained, all individually shrink-wrapped so no danger of leaving his fingerprints. He was running out of glue and calculated just two more nights work at most. He would pass that hurdle when he came to it.

The glue was a gift from one of his company jobs.

Allinn worked the lucrative weekend shift for a Worcestershire courier company. He was paid the handsome sum of £450 to be on call from 6pm Friday to 6am Monday plus 5 pence per mile for any delivery he was required to undertake.

Terry Chapman could afford him comfortably most weekends. Clients were happy to pay over the odds for out-of-hours deliveries, especially if it was as reliable and as speedy as Terry's.

One Saturday, Allinn was called away from his TV screen to deliver a kitchen specification document from a Redditch family to a house they were having renovated 20 miles away.

The family wanted to make a late amendment. The kitchen fitter had cursed at having his Saturday morning's work delayed. He was very pleased to see Allinn's bike roll up within an hour of being notified of the amendment.

Allinn had delivered to Mike Allen in the past. He invited Allinn to stay for a cup of tea but he had to crack on with the job.

"Count to five slowly," Allen said, holding up a 6ftx2ft very heavy, laminated worktop. Allinn smiled and did as he was asked. Mike Allen held the object firmly in place, stood back, counted to five himself and then slammed his clenched fist down as hard as he could on the worktop.

"Tough as old boots," he grinned.

"What is?" asked Allinn.

"This glue, pal. Best stuff I've ever seen. Only available to us pros. Of course, I still use screws and wedges but coupled with this stuff it will stick anything. And forever, so I'm told. Right, let's have a look at where Mrs Dickbrain *now* wants her freezer putting."

As the kitchen fitter was examining the designer's latest attempt to mess up HIS kitchen, Allinn gently smacked his fist against the worktop.

"Nice job," he said. "Don't suppose you'd have any of that stuff I could use? I'm doing my own kitchen soon and, sadly, I just can't afford the rates you boys charge."

"Sure, pal. Be bloody careful with it, though. I don't want to see you tearing down the road with your bloody hands stuck to those handlebars. Help yourself to a pot over there. Use it sparingly."

"Cheers, Mike."

The kitchen fitter was working away with his back to Allinn as he said goodbye, helping himself to the largest of three pots as he left.

Allinn had indeed been planning to do his kitchen...and his bathroom and his bedroom and his tiny lounge. But they were jobs for a very rainy day.

The glue pot lay unopened among a pile of assorted junk in his garage until he could find a use for it.

That day dawned at Christmastime.

Allinn had been flashed by a speed camera while returning from an infrequent long distance job. It wouldn't have been so bad if he had been using his own bike. But the package of promotional clothing for a nightclub had been bulky and Allinn had taken one of Terry Chapman's vans.

The NIP landed on the doormat at Chapman's office on New Year's Eve. Chapman was fuming. He discovered the culprit and called Allinn in to see him.

Allinn was the newest of his five employees, but Chapman did like the lad. He was polite and reliable – two qualities hard to find among some workers these days. That didn't spare Allinn from the monstering of his life.

"TWENTY-SEVEN YEARS! TWENTY-SEVEN! And not a single blemish on my licence. Call me old-fashioned but I'm quite proud of that. You...you... FUCKING idiot!"

Allinn was frozen in shock. He had never seen Chapman in a temper and certainly never heard the F word utter from his lips in the ten months he had worked for him.

Allinn was visibly shaking as he left the office. He barely managed to ride a mile before he needed to pull over. He sat quivering on a bench.

He hadn't managed to get a word in as Chapman yelled and yelled and yelled at him.

None of his drivers had ever been done before; Chapman had precious insurance policies to protect; the company had a reputation to protect; what if it got in the papers and he lost clients?

Allinn had shown Chapman his licence to prove he had no previous offences on it.

He could count himself lucky to keep his job. Naturally he would pay the fine himself. One more and he was out.

SCATE

"Happy FUCKING New Year. Now, get out of here."

Allinn had a few days off work to let things calm down. While the world partied away the start of a new year, Allinn lay on his bed listening to a forlorn Willie Nelson album. He simmered.

Still simmering, he spent New Year's Day in a miserable mood. Like Gavin Lloyd initially, he was unable to focus his anger on one particular spot. Until he stumbled upon the SCATE website. His mood brightened as he read the posts from fellow disgruntled motorists.

Eventually he signed onto the forums as Fast Eddie and posted a rant of his own. He used his real name in the private profile. But he was smart enough not to post publicly exact details of his offence – and certainly nothing that could identify Mr Chapman or his precious courier company.

He became a regular visitor at scate.co.uk. After a while he began posting locations of Gatsos in the West Midlands and surrounding areas. He now had a keen eye for them, whether making his deliveries or enjoying the late night air along deserted roads on his motorbike. He began with a simple list on his computer before graduating to databases by county, by road and, later, by his own special colour coding.

Allinn was semi-university educated. He had dropped out towards the end of a Social Studies course at Warwick. He travelled the world for 19 months, working part-time when he could. His most treasured memory was of a six-week stint in San Jose, California, where his passion for motorbikes was rekindled and he discovered a fascination for computers and the Internet.

He returned to Redditch bronzed but still as slim as ever. His brutally cropped bleached hair surprised his parents. He worked hard at a string of part-time jobs until he could afford to buy a decent bike.

Tom J Sandy

He then landed a career post with the local council, saved some more and was able to arrange a mortgage on a small flat.

The council job bored him; he considered himself to be too young to be stuck in an office handling a never-ending pile of paperwork. He jumped at the chance to join Terry Chapman's company. The salary would pay his bills, and his spending money would come from the cash he received from carrying out mechanical repairs in the garage he rented for a pittance just across from his flat.

The militant was sparked in him one morning in early February. His shift had finished and he was reading the morning paper before getting some much-needed sleep.

A brief article on two blokes being in court for torching a Gatso intrigued him.

Allinn had made his peace with Chapman by being as reliable as ever – and obeying the speed limits. Yet something inside him still simmered.

He understood the desire to strike out.

He drifted off to sleep wondering whether or not he would have the guts to torch a speed camera.

He was clearing out his garage later that same day when he decided he did have the guts, and this super glue would finally come in useful. He moved the pot to the door. Yes, he would make a mess of one of the damned things.

His first raid was two days later. He nobbled one close to home, near Bromsgrove. A simple job: he parked his bike a hundred yards away, approached the camera at an angle and quickly shattered the lens with a hammer.

He clipped a few wires and, using a kitchen knife he roughly tried to glue more wires together. He was nervous but fast. His demolition job made one paragraph in the local paper.

But it had been exhilarating, even if he had needed to fork out on a new bag. The knife had stuck to the insides and Allinn had torn the poor thing to shreds trying to remove it. Powerful stuff indeed; he would have to be more careful with it.

The first true wrecking spree and the debut appearance of Dr Glue came by chance. Allinn had been mulling over taking out a few more cameras and wondering how to leave his mark when he got a desperate call from Chapman. Would he do him a big favour and do a run to Carlisle for him? Frank's called off sick. Be ever so grateful, Kevin. I'll pay you weekend rate.

"No problems, Terry. Count on me."

He needed to deliver a CD-Rom with some important artwork on it to a Carlisle design company by 5am the day after next. He could collect the CD from a Birmingham company anytime between 3-5pm tomorrow. Someone will be expecting him at Carlisle.

"Make sure you get a signed receipt," added Chapman. "Thanks again."

"No problems, Terry. A night out on my bike...maybe I should pay you...only joking."

They shared a laugh. Things were back on a cordial footing.

Allinn had never been truly angry with Chapman; shocked by his outburst but not angry with his boss.

He had plenty of time to map out a route which would take him by a few speed cameras. He double-checked with the SCATE map and then prepared his tools. He included the cards he had designed and printed one quiet Sunday afternoon while waiting for any clients to call. The card templates were another gift from a Chapman customer, as were the picnic plates - from a client who was having a warehouse clear-out. Allinn could never turn down a free gift, no matter how useless it may seem at the time.

He slept soundly, woke late and embarked on the most exciting bike ride of his life, even his hairy trips along the Californian coast could not match the thrill he enjoyed that February night.

He collected his package shortly after 4.15pm. He loved strutting into smart offices in his leathers. He knew he stood out from other, scruffier couriers; his bleached hair made sure of that. Sadly, he was not in the mood for flirting with secretaries this particular day.

He returned home for a couple of hours to rest up. The TV was on but he wasn't paying it much attention as he double-checked his mission. Once he was completely satisfied he had laid out the best plans possible he winked at himself in the tiny mirror and headed to his garage.

He always manhandled the Yamaha out of the garage and locked the doors behind him before revving the machine for several seconds on his own road. It wasn't essential but it made the attention-seeker in him feel good. The noise was a certain head-turner.

He cruised slowly out of the 1950s estate and onto the main roads, which were still busy but easing down from the rush-hour craziness.

He was soon on the M6 and making light of the miles and the habitual traffic jams. He branched off onto a minor road in Cheshire just after 9pm, and passed several Gatsos as he neared the town of Alsager. One struck him as a suitable target; the surrounding trees were good cover. He doubled back and parked up his Yamaha. When no cars were in sight, he jogged across the road and, with heart pounding, performed his task. The first Dr Glue card had been mailed.

It wasn't the tidiest of jobs, but his dexterity would improve as the night wore on. He arrived at his Carlisle destination with 30 minutes to spare. He took off his helmet and walked up and down the street. He was smiling to himself and smoking a cheap cigar – an occasional habit. What a drive!

He handed over his package and headed back south. It was still early and there was little traffic. He took a detour around Lake Windermere and was driving through Kendal when he spotted the lights on in the Lakeland Internet Café. He enjoyed a welcome cup of coffee and a 15-minute surf around the Internet before completing his journey back to Redditch.

Too excited to sleep, he tottered around all day. There was no-one to share in his success but he celebrated all the same.

As he prepared for his third raid, he felt an inner need to have someone to share his secret hobby with. Maybe one day he would find a confidant; it was hard being an unknown hero. He was certain no-one knew his alter ego, not even those Welsh lunatics he had hung out with a couple of times.

He had already given his motorcycle its daily dose of tender loving care – he loved it almost as much as his music collection.

By 7pm he was rested and ready for an unsuspecting East Anglia. It took a little over two hours to arrive at the first camera he had noted. A possible, he thought, and drove on. He passed two more before stopping on a dirt track which skirted the road. The last one was the most inviting of the three Gatsos.

He lurked for a few minutes behind some bushes until he thought the time was ripe to make his move. There was no road lighting and no nearby houses. He donned his American-made night vision goggles and walked briskly towards the Gatso from the rear. Hammer...wire-cutters...glue on plate...firm pressure...1-2-3-4-5.

Tom J Sandy

Thank you and goodnight Newmarket. He felt that customary buzz as he roared off; nippy, but within the speed limit, of course.

There was a slight drizzle and the night air was getting chillier, but Allinn's expensive leathers protected him from the elements. The colours of his leathers and helmet matched those of his Yamaha – black with red flashes. He looked as good as he felt as he passed through Thetford and Elvedon Forest along the A11 en route to the cathedral city of Norwich.

By now Allinn had no illusions about what he was doing. None of the self-righteous pomposity spouted from the mouths of those SCATE people; he was a man of action, a modern-day adventurer with a raffish streak. He would have felt at home on the high seas a few centuries ago.

He let several promising targets pass by and then pulled into a service station on the outskirts of Norfolk's county town. He filled up the Yamaha's tank, paid for his petrol and drove round the side of the station as if to check his tyres and water. He parked away from the pressure valve, in the shadows and out of sight. He hopped over a fence and again put on his goggles. He trampled through thick, wet grass for 50 or 60 yards. The Gatso was hard to miss. It was illuminated, and set away from the trees.

Allinn crouched down, took off his goggles and quickly slipped on a pair of yellow fluorescent overalls. He skipped over a fence and looked every inch a maintenance man as he performed his task comfortably inside 15 seconds. Three cars had passed by, two on his side of the road and one opposite. They would have noticed nothing unusual. Unless they were coppers, that is – a risk I take, thought Allinn.

He climbed back over the fence, took off his overalls, replaced his goggles and made his way back to his bike. He turned left out of the service station approximately five minutes after entering it. His country needed men who possessed such military-style precision and speed. He was pleased that his forward planning had paid off. The lay-out had been exactly as he had anticipated.

He drove slowly in order to admire his handiwork and then revved up for a trip to the seaside.

He drove through the centre of Norwich to catch a glimpse of the cathedral, which he'd read was a sight worth seeing at night. Suitably impressed, he pressed on toward the main tourist attraction of the East Anglia coast – Great Yarmouth.

He had no idea what there was to do in Great Yarmouth outside the tourist season. He would imagine it was a rather desolate place. So he was frustrated by the volume of midnight traffic on the route he had mapped out down the coast. Many fortunate Gatsos escaped with their wires intact that night.

He had gone past Lowestoft before he tackled number three. His luck was back in and he was able to take out three cameras in a ten-mile stretch. All were neatly tucked away so he had no need for his overalls.

The tourist in him took another detour, this time to the quaint coastal town of Southwold – so peaceful at any time and even more so that March night. He did his best to keep the noise of the Yamaha down so as not to disturb the peace of this Olde Worlde area of natural beauty. He had fond childhood memories of the pebbly beach, the rare birds, the crazy golf course, the old-fashioned beach huts, the crumbling pier which looked to have had a decent lick of paint recently. He wondered if kids still fished for crabs across the river at Walberswick. He roused from his reveries and gathered speed on the outskirts of town. Ipswich brought back a slight gloom until he decided to risk a target by some roadworks on the south side of the town. Cars were passing by every ten seconds or so, he counted. The Gatso was brightly lit so he required his overalls.

Allinn had just finished the job and was packing away his gear when he had the shock of his life. A loud bang filled the air. A 42-ton lorry had blown a tyre. The driver appeared to have lost control and the sound of the screeching brakes filled the night.

Allinn spun around to see the lorry's headlights fixed on him. He was frozen in their beam, rooted to the spot and helplessly staring into the headlights. His breathing and his heart seemed to have stopped. The lorry was heading straight towards him. Time seemed to have stopped.

The driver somehow managed to regain control and his massive machine screeched to a halt 200 yards away after ploughing through a lane of traffic cones.

The lorry was tilted at a 45-degree angle but Allinn caught sight of the driver disembarking before he dashed back to his bike and nervously continued his journey.

The shock had made him shiver badly, much worse than any of the bike tumbles he had taken in his time.

"Close call. Close call. Bloody close call. Bloody fuckin' close call," he muttered to himself. His heart was taking its time to slow down and his nerves taking longer.

He was no longer looking out for speed cameras and several good targets passed by unnoticed.

By the time he was at Colchester he had convinced himself that if the driver had noticed anything at all in his obvious panic it would have been a curly-headed guy messing around in some bushes.

Probably having a pee.

"Always knew that wig would come in useful," Allinn chuckled to try and recover his calm. But he was shaken and he knew it. He was aware he needed to tackle another camera to fully settle his nerves; like falling off a bike, the sooner you get back on, the better.

He carefully selected a Gatso between Colchester and Braintree. It proved as simple as he had hoped.

After his next one, on the A120, he was as calm as ever. Right, just time to call in on my friend and then I'll head home.

The single SCT detective manning the Harlow HQ was struggling to stay awake. He was completely unaware that around 2am Public Vandal Number One had zipped past, just five miles away.

Allinn went through the night's events as he drove home. Eight successful missions: not bad but not as many as he had expected.

He was over his shock. In fact, the memory of it was adding to his adrenaline rush. But he was searching for a new buzz, a fresh way to torment the cops and further antagonise the politicians. He was still searching as he slipped under the covers of his welcoming bed and drifted off for eight hours sleep before his weekend shift.

Gavin Lloyd woke early and went down to the kitchen, still in his dressing gown. He had had an early night after his tiring drive back from Pete Hampson's prison.

He noticed a card lying on his doormat. It was too early for the post. He picked up the card and read:

Sorry you were out when I called. If you require attention outside office hours, please ring this number. Regards. Dr Glue.

Gavin rang the number...and got through to the Bournemouth branch of The Samaritans.

CHAPTER EIGHT

Did You See A Motorbike?

Sue came down an hour after Gavin. She was wrapped in a bath towel and rubbing her hair with a smaller one. She rarely wore much make-up but looked decidedly plain without it.

The relationship had been consummated the previous night. They had feasted on a takeaway after Gavin had returned from out west. He had told her of his trip over a few drinks. Her eyes betrayed her thoughts: they were on Gavin and not on the details of Shepton Mallet nick.

Their first kiss came during a Jim Carrey movie. They were happy to skip the end of the comedy and, giggling like two teenagers, staggered upstairs. An hour of fumbling under Gavin's sheets left them spent and deliriously happy, lying in each other's arms and wondering why they'd waited so long.

"Morning lover boy," Sue greeted him. "Well you do look distracted. What's up, darlin'?"

Gavin's mind had been a mess for the past hour. He was thinking about him and Sue and him and Dr Glue, a bizarre ménage a trois.

"We had a visitor last night," he replied and handed her the card.

"Wow!" said Sue, resting her hand on Gavin's shoulder. After a moment's silence, she added with a wink: "Shame we were busy; I'd love to meet him."

Gavin grinned. "I wonder if it was a special visit or if he was up to mischief again."

"You going to call the number?"

Gavin told her. "Suppose I'd better tell the cops. Let me scan it first." Gavin scanned the card and filed two copies on his computer hard drive: a large file and a much smaller one for possibly uploading to the website.

"You think this is how the cops got hold of the name Dr Glue?" said Sue.

"Yes. I came to that conclusion a few minutes back. Let's have a coffee and a chat then I'll try and get hold of that sergeant Wickford. Maybe you could phone Larry Evans at the same time? Then if the cops ask me to keep it quiet I can honestly claim it's too late. At least our site will have the actual card as a scoop."

"I love you," Sue kissed his cheek and put on the kettle.

Larry Evans was delighted when Sue called with another exclusive for her chosen reporter, but checked himself by hastily adding: "Hope it didn't spook Gavin."

Sue gave Evans all the details except the phone number, revealing it was a hoax number to the branch of a charity organisation.

Evans then informed Sue that he and a colleague were investigating reports of a wider outbreak of vandalism. So far they just had snaps from the Press Association. An early-bird freelance in Ipswich had managed to get some information from a decent police source. The wrecked Gatsos bore the hallmarks of the doctor.

So far Evans hadn't managed to get a response, official or unofficial, from the SCT mob.

Gavin had to settle for speaking with DS Pierce as DS Wickford was unavailable at present. Wickford was, in fact, on his way to Colchester and then Braintree to check with local police on the cameras destroyed there.

Stuart Pierce thanked Gavin for the call and hesitantly informed him that they were checking out reports of widespread wrecking.

"Keep it quiet for now, though. And don't let anyone else touch the card. We'll get someone out to see you as soon as possible. Please try and stay there until you hear from us."

"Sure thing. But it's too late about the card; my girlfriend's already handled it."

Sue had finished her conversation with Evans in time to catch the end of Gavin's call.

"*My girlfriend* – I love the sound of that."

Thankfully, Sue had a flexible role in the medical library at a Chelmsford Hospital. They arranged to have dinner together when she had returned. It was early days but both were happy they had crossed that one tricky hurdle.

ACC Hayes had arrived at work and hadn't had time to take off her coat before she heard the reports of the overnight incidents.

"Terrific! Don't you just hate boring days?" The detective constable had no time to reply to her sarcasm before she'd added: "Incident room in five minutes. Everybody. And perhaps one of our splendid examples of detection could make me a coffee."

Miserable bitch, thought DC Tony Granier. His shift had officially ended two hours ago and he needed his bed. The 26-year-old local officer was finding it hard to handle permanent night work, which he had been saddled with for the duration of the taskforce's investigations.

Before ACC Hayes had chance to address the six detectives assembled in the Incident Room, DS Pierce informed the gathering of his news from Gavin Lloyd. He'd also informed DS Wickford. Would ma'am like him to call in on the SCATE people after he'd finished his investigations in Essex?

Yes, she bloody well would. The news could have been worse –

reports of just seven wrecked cameras had come in, though there had been two unrelated incidents in Scotland. By noon the squad would hear of the Newmarket damage and were satisfied eight was the sum of Dr Glue's work that night.

"So from what we know, especially now DS Pierce has told us of the card at this Lloyd chap's home, it is our man again. No damage was done at the home, you say?"

"That's right ma'am, just a card on the mat when the guy got up this morning. Said he was in bed by midnight and up around seven o'clock. So it was sometime between then."

"And you're certain Lloyd is on the level? He doesn't know Dr Glue?"

"Well DS Wickford will no doubt press him further on that when he calls later today. But from what we know already I would say he's telling the truth. Everything those SCATE people do would go up in smoke if we proved any connection."

"Who's checking the other cases today?"

"Just DS Wickford from here, ma'am. Tony contacted him first thing as he knew he lived nearby. Local liaison officers are handling the others, and they realise how keen we are on forensics."

"The Norwich forensic people are examining one as we speak, ma'am," interrupted DC Granier, pleased that sergeant Pierce had given him a name-check in front of the ACC. "They were the first to call in this morning. It seems a guy walking his dog spotted it. Sadly, his dabs will be on it. They did confirm there was a card stuck inside. I have no details on that yet."

ACC Hayes grunted. "Can't wait to hear his latest wit and wisdom. Any news on the teams outside?"

It was the turn of DS Williams to speak. Sarah Williams was a 33-

SCATE

year-old mother-of-two who had worked with ACC Hayes at Southend on several cases. Her colleagues had dubbed her DS Glue. Her role was to try and trace those responsible for the distribution of the glue within the UK. It was a thankless task.

"Not much, I'm afraid, ma'am. The preliminary work done by Lancashire Police has helped speed things up but it's going to take time to get round all those involved. We have narrowed the search down a bit, however.

"So far we have confirmation from Singapore that they ship to 38 firms here. Twenty-six of those importers treat the glue before it is passed on and from samples taken we are certain our man's supply came from one of those.

"Problem is the next line in the chain involves more than 350 outlets, mainly wholesalers. They will have thousands of clients. We'll keep checking but, to be frank, I'm not hopeful."

"The surprising thing is we have not one eye-witness yet, ma'am," said DS Pierce. "No word on what this guy looks like and nothing on the motor he's using. I was wondering if it might be time for an appeal?"

ACC Hayes slowly nodded as she appeared deep in thought. "Fair enough. Let's see what today brings and if necessary I'll make an announcement to the great British public tomorrow lunchtime. I'll let you know before I leave tonight whether or not to inform the Press. Back to work, then."

The meeting closed and ACC Hayes walked over to a row of computers to check the latest news and reports. She read a brief item from Suffolk Police.

The Newmarket Clerk Of The Course had reported seeing a damaged speed camera while on his way to the racetrack. It was being checked out but the force was always over-burdened on race days.

DS Wickford had decided to pay Gavin Lloyd a call before letting HQ know of his possible new lead.

By sheer chance, he had heard two officers in Colchester poking fun at the poor buggers stuck in a two-mile traffic jam in rush-hour on the Ipswich by-pass. A lorry had shattered the carefully laid-out cones and smashed a builder's gantry; right by that bashed-up Gatso, they chuckled. Clearly these officers were no friends of the British motorist, nor of the Government's camera policy, thought Wickford.

"The driver was in a worse state than the road, according to Fred Dobbs," said one. "Thought he'd killed some bloke having a piss in the bushes."

"Stupid bloody place to stop for a leak," added the other.

Wickford interrupted their raw humour and was given the number of Fred Dobbs – the best guy to contact at Ipswich.

Dobbs had finished his shift when Wickford got around to phoning. But a fellow officer was happy to provide a number for the driver.

"Sorry, Mrs Vaughan, but, yes, it really is important I speak to your Stevie now. Don't worry, he's not in any trouble," DS Wickford informed the wife of the Clacton lorry driver.

A sleepy Stevie Vaughan told DS Wickford that he had told the copper at the station everything he could about his accident. He wasn't doing anything wrong, a tyre just blew out that's all.

"Yes, I realise that Mr Vaughan. Nothing for you to worry about at all," DS Wickford was at his reassuring best.

"I am hoping you can help us with another important matter. You told the officer at Ipswich that when your tyre blew out you had to struggle to control your vehicle and to avoid hitting a pedestrian.

Can you tell me anything about this person? Anything at all may be most helpful."

"Well I was shocked as you can imagine. The lorry swung to the right and I was trying to drag it back onto my side of the road when I saw this face in the headlights. I only got a brief glimpse of him but he was deathly white and his eyes were so wide. It was like he was frozen.

"I nearly crapped myself and wasn't sure if I had hit him. But I managed to get the lorry pretty much straight and edged into the side. Sent a good few of those cones flying. It was the most frightening moment of my life. I got out of the cab and, well, I was sick...but I did go back to where the guy had been and saw no-one there. That was a relief, I can tell you."

"This was by a speed camera, right?"

"Errm, yes, I'm sure it was by one of those bloody things...didn't hang around there long. I ran back to my lorry and phoned in."

"Can you remember what he was wearing? You say he was white?"

"Yes, white as a ghost. He was wearing very dark clothes. Sorry, I wasn't really concentrating on him...more on getting the lorry straight. Oh, he did have something by his arm, a helmet maybe."

"A motorbike helmet?"

"Yes I think so. Wouldn't like to swear on it."

"Did you see a motorbike?"

"No, just the bloke."

"Thanks very much, Mr Vaughan. Can you do me a favour and jot down this number – and if you remember anything about this man – anything at all – please get in touch with me or one of my colleagues immediately. Once again, this has nothing to do with your accident and you are not in any trouble. Sorry for disturbing your sleep but you have been most helpful."

It was just after noon when DS Wickford arrived at Gavin's home. The web master had just finished loading the Dr Glue card onto the home page of the SCATE site. He blacked out the phone number just in case any site visitors decided to disturb the good work of the Bournemouth Samaritans.

He'd written a story to accompany the photo exclusive. Highlighted in red was a footnote proclaiming that neither he nor any of the SCATE members knew the identity of Dr Glue nor did they condone his acts of vandalism. He had also added a link to the Evening Standard story on the wreckage caused the previous night.

"Hello, Sergeant Wickford, I've been expecting you. Come in. Fancy a coffee?"

"Thank you, Mr Lloyd, that would be welcome. Four sugars, please. Got to keep myself sweet for the missus. May I see this card then?" Gavin let DS Wickford study the card as he dealt with the coffees.

"Yes, it's our doctor," confirmed the detective.

"So, he's left more of these around, then?" said Gavin.

DS Wickford could have kicked himself. Of course, Lloyd wasn't aware of the others.

Over the course of the conversation, DS Wickford revealed, in the strictest confidence, that Dr Glue had left his calling card here and there. He discovered it was too late to stop this particular case getting into the Press. Sue had already told the Evening Standard, who were running with the story.

"Wish you hadn't done that without checking with us, sir," frowned DS Wickford. "Still, too late now.

"About last night, do you have any idea what time you had this surprise visit?"

"Between going to bed around midnight and getting up just after seven I guess."

"Did you hear anything in the night? The letterbox? Footsteps on the path? The sounds of a car? Or maybe...a motorbike?"

"No, nothing." Not that a thermo-nuclear explosion could have disturbed he and Sue.

"And you're sure, absolutely certain, that you don't know this man?"

"Yes. I told you the truth last time you called. I'm assuming this is a dig at us and our *peaceful* protests. By the way, was your boss interested in putting the police view on the web site?"

"Yes, she was very interested, and we should have something for you soon. Is there anything else you can tell me that has happened since we last spoke?"

"Afraid not. I've asked our members and they don't have a clue who he is."

"OK. Thanks for calling us. I'll take the card, unless you have any objections. Keep in touch."

By mid-afternoon DS Wickford had the rapt attention of ACC Hayes.

"So, you're pretty convinced this guy who was scared witless is our man?"

"It's the only lead we have; unless any other ID's have come in overnight?"

"No they haven't. Nothing. Amazing, really, as some of the cameras have been in open view on busy roads – even at the absurd hours he keeps. But I don't want to go clutching at straws for the sake of it. I trust you, Steve. What's your gut feeling?"

"Yes, I think it is him. Not enough to bet my mortgage on it, but it's the best lead we have."

"Right, let's run with it softly for now, and let's keep the details within HQ until the morning. The liaison officers just need to know we have a *possible* sighting of a white male wearing dark clothing. He was *possibly* riding a motorcycle. See if they get anywhere with a few discreet enquiries around the damaged sites. Good work."

"Thanks, ma'am. Just one other thing; the girlfriend of our SCATE contact told a friend of hers on the Evening Standard about the card."

"Yes, I'm told it made today's edition. The Press Office has been instructed to stonewall inquiries pending a Press Conference."

"Press Conference?"

"Nothing's finalised, but I've pencilled one in for the morning; just in case we have any information to divulge or to ask eye-witnesses to come forward. Let's see how the motorcyclist angle works out first."

There would be a Press Conference the following day. But not headed by ACC Hayes at the SCT offices.

Dr Glue had the tabloid papers at war and a handsome cheque from the Daily Mirror had uncovered details of a Midlands police chief's wife escaping a speeding penalty.

Her car had been flashed doing 85mph through road works in a 50-zone.

The long arm of the Masons yielded some free legal advice. She claimed she wasn't driving the car on the evening in question and for the life of her had no idea who would have been.

The red-faced superintendent insisted his wife had done nothing wrong and it had been entirely up to the traffic police to decide whether to proceed with the prosecution. If there was a loophole, it was up to the Government to close it.

SCATE

There was no loophole, the Government stressed in the House of Commons the following Monday afternoon. It was the responsibility of the driver to provide police with correct details on who was driving the vehicle or face the charge him or herself.

Sean Chapman was on the back-foot, even backbenchers from his own party had difficulty cheering on their transport secretary as he reeled under the onslaught from Caroline Mitchell.

Thankfully, his Prime Minister was away on some foreign jaunt and was not present to witness Chapman's embarrassment.

Once Mitchell had again reiterated her party's total condemnation of vandalism.

"Wasn't this Government elected on the promise of tackling crime and the *causes* of crime? Wasn't the Government's policy the *cause* of these particular crimes?"

Mutterings from the Government benches, wild cheering from the Tory side of the House – many backbenchers had been called upon to reply to angry constituents on the subject of these invidious cameras.

Mitchell continued: "Could the Right Honourable Member update the House on the latest cost of providing replacement cameras? Lest he think this side of the House is simply concerned with the treasury's coffers, could he also provide details of how many police man-hours had been wasted chasing these *criminals*?"

Gasps greeted the figures that Chapman revealed; unfortunately he did not have to hand figures on the police time.

"But let no-one be mistaken, this Government backs the police force wholeheartedly in its fight against crime and will continue to provide whatever funding is necessary..."

Groans forced the transport secretary to again yield to Mitchell.

"All well and good, but this Government needs to understand that what the people want is bobbies back on the beat; on the street beat and on the traffic beat. The last thing they want is silly initiatives from a Government that is...dead beat."

Her closing comments on her Party's pledges were all but drowned out in hysterical laughter. Caroline Mitchell sat down, feeling like she had just scored the winner in the Cup Final. She possessed neither the intellect nor the drive of Margaret Thatcher, but this daughter of Lincolnshire also aimed to make her mark in politics.

That evening, the SCATE members gathered around Gavin's table. They heard the regular updates from all, but were assembled to make plans for their biggest demonstration yet.

They discussed the card Dr Glue had delivered to Gavin's door and threatened untold violence if he ever got rough with them. They were worried about the emerging message boards, and not because they saw them as rivals to the SCATE boards. These were run by self-styled men of action, not words. Most of the action men had already been taken in by the law. But, like suicide bombers, there seemed no shortage of fresh volunteers.

Neil Proust had had several thousand leaflets and posters printed at cost. The leaflets were to be distributed at a select band of football ground the next Saturday.

"For God's sake make sure they don't get stuck under car windscreen wipers; drivers hate that," said Frank McIvor. "Love the posters, much better than my lot made."

The posters were indeed quite humourous. A picture of a speed camera warning with the wording suitably altered:

Please Make Cheques Payable To The Chief Constable

SCATE

I'm Hungry! Please Feed Me £60.
Feel Free To Drink And Drive Past Me

The group rapidly dismissed the notion of pasting them over the official warning signs: that would smack of Dr Glue and would probably land them in hot water with the cops. Make great placards for their group outing to Aintree, though.

So they firmed up their schedule for Grand National Day. They had a dozen or so volunteers to help their peaceful protest at the biggest race day in Britain. Sue had booked the party into a hotel. Sadly, she informed the other four, the best deal she could find was 25 miles away.

"These may come in useful," said J.J. The others had noticed him fiddling with something under the table.

He stood up and made loud trumpeting sounds before revealing the object of his attention.

"May have a test run at the Boat Race next weekend," he grinned.

CHAPTER NINE

Highland Fling

Kevin Allinn was coming to the end of a moderately-busy weekend stint on the road, ferrying documents and a few small packages around the West Midlands with one trip out to Wales.

On his way home he'd stopped off at Llandrindrod Wells and called in for a cuppa with Rhys Williams, one of the few anti-Gatso Welshmen he'd got on with.

No, Rhys wasn't hanging out with the old crowd much these days. They'd learned from poor Pete Hampson's escapade and didn't fancy joining him inside. He'd never got round to visiting Pete, but he had sent him a letter and always asked Jonesy to pass on his best wishes. Chris Jones did pop down to Shepton Mallet nick whenever he could.

At their height, the Welsh boys were a crazy crew. They once deliberately sped past a camera, three of the men exposing themselves through their van's rear window. Sensibly, they had masked the number plate.

They had torched a few, bulldozed one, and smashed the occasional lens.

"Still, this Dr Glue seems to have the bloody cops on the hop. Doing a better job than any of us could, eh? Hope he takes care not to get caught."

"Yeah! That guy's a regular superstar. Don't worry, Rhys. He won't get caught."

And with a sly wink, Kevin Allinn was back on his bike. He stopped off at an Internet café in Leominster, grabbed a sandwich and left a short note on one of the SCATE boards:

Running out of glue...need help. No hoaxers please. You can contact me on the following number during normal office hours.

And he left the number of the switchboard at ACC Hayes's HQ.

The flurry of calls that hit the SCT switchboard on the Monday morning made up ACC Hayes's mind. She knew it was risky but she had to go public. The discreet enquiries had brought forth no further information on the man almost killed by Steve Vaughan's lorry. She called a Press Conference for the next morning.

The police wanted to question – if only to eliminate from their enquiries – a white male who was seen in the early hours of March 18th on the A45 near Ipswich, she informed the reporters, who were desperate for any fresh information to pad out their slender stories. He was possibly a motorcyclist.

Possibly? The hacks queried. Hadn't they any clearer idea?

"That is all we are prepared to reveal for now," she replied haughtily, as if keeping a secret close to her chest. "Our enquiries are continuing. I would like to remind the public of the special hotline we have set up so they can provide any information in the strictest confidence.

"Let me remind you all; this vandal is putting lives at risk and preventing the police doing the job it is paid to do. Thank you for your attendance today."

One hundred and thirty miles apart, Allinn and Gavin Lloyd listened to the Press Conference broadcast on BBC Radio 5 Live.

A biker, mused Gavin. He had expected some man in a van.

Allinn's reaction was fearful at first. So, he had been clocked that night. Where? And by whom? Could have been the lorry driver. Didn't think he'd have had the time or the frame of mind to memo-

SCATE

-rise anything. The cops didn't appear to have much to go on, thankfully. They weren't even sure if I was on a bike. That bit did puzzle him, 'possibly a motorcyclist', AAC Hayes had said.

He had been pondering his next campaign since the previous day. His note at scate.co.uk had been true. He was running out of glue, and he could hardly call up the kitchen fitter and ask for more; he had taken his largest tub of the lovely stuff.

He flicked through the weekend papers once more before hitting the sack.

When he woke he plotted his final outing as Dr Glue. Scotland deserved a visit, he had decided. He booked a flight for early Wednesday morning from Birmingham to Edinburgh at a nice price.

He was unfamiliar with the roads between Edinburgh and Glasgow but did know they presented plenty of opportunities. He spent most of Monday night and all day Tuesday pouring over maps and checking the placement of Gatsos with the scate.co.uk map.

He decided to check-in the rucksack containing his equipment, even though it probably could have passed as hand luggage. He didn't want to risk a spot check at the gate and decided the hold was safer for his bag of tricks.

He paid for an expensive coffee on the flight. So this was how no-frills airlines made their money.

At Edinburgh airport he found the cheapest car rental company and found just what he was seeking: a dark blue Ford Escort would be fine. Yes, just for the one day, please. I'll have it back around 5am tomorrow morning.

He drove with the driver's window down and enjoyed the Scottish air on a bright March day. The slight chill would not bother a hardy biker like Kevin Allinn. He pulled into a lay-by, and once certain there was no-one in his line of vision he smeared a thin coat of transparent varnish over front and rear registration plates. All would appear normal to the naked eye, yet a Gatso would be screened. He coated his Yamaha at least once a fortnight.

He enjoyed several touristy hours in the Scottish capital and, as so often before on his travels, told himself it was worthy of a proper visit one day. Then he drove the 45 miles to Glasgow along the M8. He clocked up 79 miles with his detours to check out several potential targets.

He wolfed down a burger and dozed off during an early evening movie in Clydebank. He returned to his car and rested for half an hour until he was satisfied the time was ripe.

Allinn enjoyed the comfort of the Escort but missed the buzz of his bike. He listened to a radio phone-in and smiled as football fans called for the heads of managers up and down the land.

This would be Dr Glue's shortest journey, yet his most profitable. There were two Gatsos close together in Clydebank so it would be inconsiderate not to start his night's work with a double whammy. He parked by a noisy pub and covered the half-mile between both on foot, neat work and no need to don his overalls.

He was delighted to achieve two more doubles that night. Detours took him to Airdrie, Motherwell and Whitburn. He was using the glue more sparingly and managed to wreck 15 speed cameras in four hours and 25 minutes. The easiest night yet, he thought, as he dumped the empty glue pot in a skip near Dalkeith.

"So long, old friend," he told it. "We had fun along the way, didn't we?"

He parked up in the car rental bay at the airport and dozed a while until it was time for his flight home. Before returning to his flat,

SCATE

Allinn stopped off at the Metropole hotel in Birmingham. It was always hectic at breakfast time. He logged onto a computer and posted to the SCATE board:

Dr Glue is dead. Long live the son of Dr Glue.

Within two hours of his post, two SCT liaison officers were quizzing staff at the Metropole. Sorry, they didn't notice anyone with a motorcycle helmet; breakfast was their busiest time, you have to understand.

It was early in the afternoon before ACC Hayes and her team were aware of the full extent of the rampage.

"And what are we to make of his message? Son of Dr Glue?" ACC Hayes asked her officers.

"A new MO maybe, ma'am?" suggested DS Wickford. "Follows on from his message about running out of glue. Could be just another of his pranks, of course."

"Well keep plugging away at the glue angle. I know it's a long shot but we never know. Any *good* news on the forensic front from Scotland?"

The silence told its own story.

"Anything else, anyone?"

"Just an observation, ma'am, but his four raids so far have all been mid-week and late at night."

"And pray what does that tell us DS Williams? He likes to keep his weekends free?"

Sarah Williams recognised the sarcasm in her chief's voice. It usually meant she was rattled.

"Could mean he works weekends, ma'am," she replied hesitantly.

"The Birmingham lads have asked the Metropole to keep an eye out for anyone suspicious, ma'am. That appears to be the only place he has used twice to send messages. But they checked the dates against the guest lists and there is no match," said DS Pierce. "So it looks like a public visitor."

"Someone who lives in the Birmingham area, or who passes through on business?" said DC Granier.

"What about the motorcycle angle?" asked DS Alex Scott. "He must have been going some to get from Edinburgh to Birmingham in six hours or so."

"Piece of piss on a good bike," snapped DS Wickford, "especially at that time of day."

They were trying to make up a composite picture of their villain. But they had so little to go on. Wickford's lorry driver and his scared witless white male who was possibly carrying a motorcycle helmet was their only real lead.

The meeting broke up, officers went in search of their unknown villain while ACC Hayes composed a memo for the equally-beleaguered transport secretary.

Thirty-two Gatsos had been wrecked in the past six days – 15 of them the work of Dr Glue. Three culprits had been apprehended and charged. The SCATE group was organising a demo at the Grand National; naturally police would have spotters out. Regretfully, she had no further information on Dr Glue for the Secretary of State.

The National was several days away. J.J. had a mission of his own to complete the weekend before, a day at the Boat Race.

One of his many business acquaintances had come up with another sure-fire winner. He had had 2,000 inflatable plastic Gatsos made and was planning to distribute them to traders along the Essex coast. J.J. persuaded his friend to hand over 200 at cost – cash, of course – and got him to agree to delay his distribution until Easter.

SCATE

"They'll be in the news by then, and you'll make a killing. Wait and see. The holiday-makers will snap 'em up."

J.J. drove into London with one of his occasional lady friends early on Sunday morning.

"You know how to treat a girl," said Naomi Lockwood as J.J. parked his BMW as close to Chiswick Bridge as he could.

"Oh, you're honoured," laughed J.J. "Don't think I bring all the Romford ladies on such wild adventures. Fancy a drink first? We can come back for our gear."

Naomi was a 30-year-old, intelligent, dark-haired, pretty woman who had known J.J. through their local pub for almost five years. Never married but with a string of casual boyfriends behind her, Naomi hated the image of Essex girl. Because she enjoyed a good time it didn't make her an airhead blonde, did it?

She drove a Fiat Punto, but preferred public transport except when doing her fortnightly supermarket grind. She had never been troubled by a speed camera, and had no interest in SCATE and all that nonsense.

She liked J.J., however. And she had never been to the Boat Race.

The Boat Race was a great British tradition dating back to 1829 when two students mooted the idea of a challenge between the universities of Oxford and Cambridge.

More a social occasion than a mighty sporting event, the race always attracted huge crowds and live television coverage.

The banks of the River Thames were densely packed, pubs did a roaring trade and two often American-dominated crews grunted and sweated over a four-and-a-quarter-mile course for the glory of Britain's finest seats of learning.

"I must be a daft as you," said Naomi over a glass of white wine. "We just stand there and wave those silly things all the time?"

"Not all the time, just when the boats are at the finishing line. I won't embarrass you to join me in running down to greet the winning team."

Naomi had little to worry about. They did manage to get a front row position by the bridge at the finishing line. The TV images, however, were too distant to make out the details of the inflatables this crazy couple were waving.

The next morning's paper, though, did carry photos on their inside pages. Three papers used an agency photo of a blond-haired man, grinning as the beefy Cambridge crew passed him. He had an inflatable Gatso in one hand and a placard in the other. It featured a camera logo and read:

Ain't You Glad The Thames Is A Gatso-Free Zone?

Naturally, the photo made the SCATE website. A day later they began selling inflatables online. J.J.'s entrepreneurial pal was delighted and ordered another batch from an equally-happy manufacturer.

They would be out in force at Aintree.

Gavin Lloyd had difficulty concentrating on planning the demos that week. His mind was elsewhere, hunting Kevin Allinn.

Alerted by Pete Hampson's cryptic letter, he had checked the SCATE site and discovered a Kevin Allinn had signed up to the forums as 'Fast Eddie'. His private profile revealed he lived in the West Midlands. He had used a hotmail email address.

Gavin discovered that Fast Eddie had ceased posting three days before Dr Glue emerged.

He told Sue when she had risen from her slumber. She was spending several nights a week with Gavin by now, usually when the chil-

-dren were at their mother's house. They had discussed their future and decided to take things gradually. Gavin was certain Jim and Kate would accept Sue's entrance into their family with no fuss.

Sue was excited enough to cancel a shopping expedition and walk with her boyfriend to the local library. They had had no luck searching for a 'Kevin Allinn' online.

The library proved successful. Allinn was not a common name.

"Thank the Lord we aren't looking for a Smith," Sue joked as the couple sat down at a desk. A huge pile of telephone directories hid them from the book browsers. They decided to make notes on all the Allinns and went home with a list of 12. Two of them were K Allinns. One lived in Wolverhampton, the other in Redditch.

Once home they were unsure what to do next. They re-read his five posts at the forums. There was nothing unusual about them. He appeared to be just another motorist in a rage at being Gatso'd. He claimed to have almost lost his job because of his offence.

They checked the IP addresses against those used by Dr Glue; nothing there to arouse suspicion. They checked the content of his posts and the style against the doctor's. Some of the language used was consistent. Then Sue stumbled upon two phrases which matched: *I've had a bellyful of these cameras.'*

"Not a particularly uncommon expression," she said. "Interesting to see it used by two different users, though."

"Must be him," said Gavin.

"Whatcha gonna do? Call the cops?"

Gavin told of his promise to Pete Hampson. Sue was surprised he had agreed to Hampson's deal but secretly pleased. They decided to sit on the information until meeting the others at the hotel on Friday.

Kevin Allinn nagged at Gavin all week, but he pressed on with his preparations for the big day out at the races.

He had a meeting with MP Humphrey Bellow who passed on his leader's regards and wished them well for their protest, as long as it is peaceful, he emphasised.

Caroline Mitchell would have a piece ready for the website within a day or so. Had he received anything yet from Sean Chapman? Gavin had had no reply either way from the transport secretary.

He had, however, been granted an article from ACC Hayes. Well, the assistant chief constable had signed it but he was certain it was penned by a traffic officer.

He fielded a check phone call from DS Wickford. Yes, Gavin was bemused by the 'Son of Dr Glue' message and would let the police know if any information turned up.

The police were primed for the appearance of the doctor in whatever guise he chose. ACC Hayes had increased manning levels for the overnight mid-week shifts. Forces throughout Britain were warned to have officers ready to react immediately to news of any vandalised cameras.

Dr Glue was taking a week off. Or, more accurately, his son was.

Kevin Allinn had bought a Peugeot 205 van from one of his boss's customers. A good runner, just needed some minor attention. It was a snip at eight hundred quid.

Allinn was fixing the Peugeot up in his garage. It would be ready and raring to go on a raid next week.

When the weekend arrived, Alison Hayes was relieved that there had been no further raids. The extra manpower costs were no concern of hers, better to be prepared. Several chief constables did express their reservations, however, to the transport secretary. They were informed in no uncertain terms that the Government backed the SCT to the hilt.

Sean Chapman was worried about costs, even if he kept his fears to himself. He had had a quiet week on the political front. But a shiver went down his spine when he read the details of the surveillance teams ACC Hayes was sending to Aintree. He could estimate the costs himself.

He steeled himself for more angry correspondence from chief constables and another mauling at the hands of that cow Caroline Mitchell if the police didn't find this vandal soon.

"Fancy a go on the sweep, sir? Fiver a time."

Chapman glowered at the civil servant but pulled £10 out of his wallet.

"Two goes, sir?"

"No, I'd like change, please."

He received his change and picked a slip of paper from the bowler hat proffered by the civil servant.

"Radio Zombie. A 33-1 shot, sir. Has a decent chance if the ground stays good to firm. Christine is holding the money until Monday morning. First four wins a prize. Good luck."

Get out of here, you chirpy bastard, thought Chapman. But he maintained the dignity expected of a member of Laurence Carr's cabinet and muttered: "Fingers crossed then, and good luck to all."

There was only one horse Kevin Allinn could put his money on as he entered the bookies on National day. A rank 150-1 outsider, but Allinn decided his tenner each way would ride on *Camera Shy*.

CHAPTER TEN

A Day At The Races

The Grand National had a history almost as old as the Boat Race. After The Beatles, it was Liverpool's most famous export.

People gambled millions on the world's most famous steeplechase race every year; people who would normally never dream of entering a bookie's shop. Workplaces held their own sweepstakes.

You owned part of a horse for a day. You may have chosen it at random, or after studying yards and yards of detailed form guides.

Six hundred million people worldwide would be glued to their television sets for the nine or ten minutes it took the jockeys to guide their steeds around the four-and-a-half-mile course.

Many of the 40 horses would not last the punishing race over the most daunting fences in racing. Some horses would lose their lives. It is a very strange sporting day. There is a romance about it that grips the British people.

It was also ideal for publicity-seekers, fanatics and even terrorists. An IRA bomb threat once caused the race to be postponed for two days.

Of the SCATE members among the 70,000 spectators at Aintree that Saturday, only Frank McIvor was a true racing man.

McIvor had been happy to pass on his expert knowledge to his friends over drinks at their hotel. "Of course, it's a bloody lottery, really," he added.

"Want a red-hot inside tip?" said Sue.

Of course they all did.

"Don't gamble!" she added cheekily, then admitted she would have a fiver each-way on some nag with three legs.

The group ran through details of their plan of action for race day. The previous weekend thousands of leaflets had been distributed at football grounds. Then, of course, there had been J.J.'s outing by the riverside. All congratulated him on his Boat Race triumph.

When they were satisfied they had covered everything, Gavin revealed his big news.

Without mentioning Pete Hampson's letter, he told J.J., McIvor and Neil Proust he had a possible clue to the identity of Dr Glue.

He told them of the research done by him and Sue. What did the group think they should do?

To Gavin's relief none suggested informing the police.

J.J. spoke first. "Part of me thinks he's a riot. He's given us all a bloody good laugh. But I just think he's making the Government dig its heels in. There's no way they'll back down on the Gatsos if it could be seen as a victory for a vandal. That Sean Chapman's such a pompous tosser."

"I agree. But, yeah, I have to admit I have a grudging admiration for the guy," admitted McIvor. "Dr Glue, I mean...not that pompous tosser, as you so beautifully put it."

"Me, too," nodded Proust. "But if we wanted to go out and nobble a few dozen cameras we could do it, no problems. I know guys who could probably take out a couple of hundred in a week and not get caught."

"Exactly, Neil. I was wondering if your friends may be able to help us out?" said Gavin.

"You mean make a house call?" said Neil. "I'm sure that could be arranged. How many did you say you'd narrowed it down to?"

Sue produced a copy of the list.

"Right, makes sense to start with the two K. Allinns and work from there. I'll get onto it after the race. No questions, OK? It'll be taken care of. No violence, I promise. Friendly persuasion can work wonders."

They all knew not to probe too deeply into Proust's network of contacts. And they trusted the tough Tyke implicitly.

As they prepared to retire for the night, J.J. slapped his hands on the shoulders of Gavin and Sue.

"We are a couple now, I gather; very pleased to hear it. You're a diamond pair. See you in the morning."

McIvor and Proust polished off their breakfasts at breakneck speed. The others nibbled and were happy to let the two northern lads help themselves to extras from their plates.

J.J. and McIvor drove the two rented mini-coaches to the service station where they had arranged to pick up their volunteers. Two more than anticipated had shown up and were vouched safe by their friends. Fortunately they had bought their own tickets.

They spent a few minutes that chill April morning exchanging pleasantries and introducing each other.

All were known to at least one member of the group by sight. One couple had been on McIvor's demos, three had enjoyed Gavin's hospitality in Essex. They were in regular email contact or posted frequently on the SCATE boards.

Gavin ran through their objectives for the day. The leaflets were to be handed out at the entrance. The plastic Gatsos and balloons – another J.J. scheme – were to be inflated once they were on the racetrack. They had decided against placards as they would probably be confiscated as dangerous objects.

They were assigned best-visibility areas of the racetrack for TV coverage: the start and finish lines, the fences at Beecher's Brook and Valentines, the winners' enclosure.

"J.J. knows what he's doing, don't you, J.J.?"

"Sure do, Gavin. As the prettiest one here I'm ready for my close-up," he laughed.

"Neil will keep a low profile as he's naturally shy. But he will be on hand if anyone needs him. What do you keep looking at, Neil?" Proust had been glancing over his shoulder.

"A couple in that red Mondeo over there. The guy keeps pointing a camera our way. Our friendly police force, I assume. Let's have one of your business cards, Gavin, and I'll go and say hello."

The couple pretended to be reading a map as Proust walked towards their vehicle.

"Can I help you? You look lost," said Proust, friendly as could be.

"No, we're fine, thanks mate," replied the guy, his eyes betraying fright at the imposing figure staring through his window.

"Good. Let us know if any of your snaps come out. We're always on the look-out for contributors. You can send them here." Proust flicked Gavin's card through the window and wished the couple a nice day.

"Nothing to worry about," Proust told the unlikely group of protesters. "I guess we should expect some attention today."

By 10am the group was handing out leaflets to early arrivals at Aintree. Many were simply discarded by people with nothing on their minds but a good time at the races and maybe, just maybe, a tiny profit. Yet there was a pleasing number of well-wishers. One middle-aged, smartly dressed man even spent ten minutes helping distribute leaflets. He told them he'd been flashed twice; before he had to run. "Essential to study the form, you know."

They were inside the racecourse by noon and handing out balloons. "Don't give them to kids unless their parents ask," Gavin had warned. "Don't want anyone getting stroppy."

It wasn't easy walking around the course. Gavin had been racing several times previously but the crowds at Newmarket were nothing like this. Sue was a racing virgin and expressed shock at the sight of some of the fences.

"You mean they actually jump over that thing?" she said as they gazed at The Chair.

"A tough, old game," replied Gavin. "Rather them than me."

The first race flew by. TV showed fleeting images of the inflatables at various sections around the course. The faces of two McIvor pals were just about discernible at the finishing line.

J.J. made his debut before the third race. The star of the Boat Race squeezed his slight frame into prime position just behind the Bookie Basher.

The eccentric TV tipster was explaining to his mass audience why his selection in the last race had failed so miserably. But, look on the bright side, Diamond Joe is a very decent price for the next one, folks, and has been impressing his connections on the gallops. TV caught a clear shot of J.J. among the face-pulling throng behind the Bookie Basher. He sported a white tee-shirt with a speed camera on it, and underneath the slogan:

Save £60 for
the journey
home – you
may need it

J.J. spotted a dark-suited 30-ish man staring at him as he went to the gents toilet. But he was back behind the Bookie Basher for the build-up to the big race. He was wearing a new tee-shirt for the entertainment of the nation. This one sported a photo of transport secretary Sean Chapman, suitably doctored to make his features look like a crazed cartoon character. The slogan read:

I'm having £60

On Camera Shy

No! Make

That £70!

The BBC producers allowed J.J. almost 45 seconds of glory before one of their lackeys gently moved him on.

It was proving a good day for the SCATE crowd. Some people did actually read their leaflets, some even stuffed them in their pockets, a couple of hundred balloons flew in the gentle breeze, one of the TV reporters commented on their inflatables and a pundit chipped in that he'd been flashed by one of the ruddy things on his way home from Catterick races. "You were flashed by an inflatable?" teased the reporter. The frown from the racing expert persuaded her to rapidly change subject.

The only blot on the day for those foolhardy with their money was the abysmal showing of Camera Shy. It fell at the The Chair along with three other horses.

None of the protesters had backed the winner, 25-1 shot Youvegottalaugh, but McIvor was pleased with the small return on his selection, which managed to hold onto fourth place.

They had plenty of time to discuss their day in the traffic jams out of Aintree. They jeered as they drove past a Gatso at a stately 15mph.

Several members of the group had spotted a few strange looks from people in the crowd, but no-one had seen any cameras trained on them, not even Neil Proust.

Well, except for Sue's camera – she had taken more than a hundred photos with her new Canon digital.

J.J. again made the papers, He'd spoken briefly to a couple of news reporters and he featured in the news reports of the grand occasion. Shame the photo was a fuzzy image grabbed from a video of the BBC coverage.

There was also a good shot of two inflatables at the finishing line as Youvegottalaugh claimed the great prize for its Cumbrian owner.

The SCATE members dropped their volunteers off at the service station and returned to the hotel. Proust promised to make some calls next week. He was confident they would trace this Kevin Allinn.

McIvor would be down south soon, he hoped, and would drop by.

They went their separate ways. Gavin and J.J. drove the two rented vans back to Romford. Sue made J.J. happy by sharing half the journey with him. She refused to tell him how many children her and Gavin planned to have.

It was almost noon on the Sunday after the race when Gavin settled down to his website work. He had to report on the success at Aintree and answer a larger than usual crop of emails.

It took him an hour to sift through Sue's photos. He selected 48 for the site and ensured that all of the volunteers were in view. He wrote a brief report of his own and made links to several news sites.

Two of his emails stood out. One was from the personal secretary of Samuel Owens. The Tory leader wished to congratulate him and his friends on their successful peaceful protest – a fine example of democracy at work. Rather formal, but a nice gesture, thought Gavin.

The other was much warmer and came from the hand of Caroline Mitchell rather than her secretary. Gavin had yet to meet the Tory transport spokeswoman but immediately warmed to her style.

Best laugh she'd had in ages. And she wondered if she could buy one of that blond chap's tee-shirts? She needed a new one for gardening. If our Humphrey ever gets round to inviting you to Westminster it would be a pleasure to meet you. Keep up the good work.

"Friends in high places, indeed," said Sue.

Kevin Allinn had few real friends. His work saw to that. He had many casual acquaintances down the pub. But, basically, he was a loner and liked it that way most of the time.

Allinn never got to see Camera Shy fall in the National as he was out on a job. He read the next day's papers with amusement as he awaited clients.

That SCATE crowd had had a fun day, it seemed. Soft bastards would never get anywhere, though; Allinn was certain of that.

He had the right idea: put *real* pressure on the Government. It may take some time but he was convinced they would back down. Of course he realised it would be on their own terms. They could not be seen to be caving in to outlaws like him. If they had any sense they would cease erecting Gatsos without any fuss, and just forget to replace the ruined ones. Well, that made absolute sense to Allinn.

He was also plotting the debut of Dr Glue's son. The van was ready and Allinn would be by Tuesday. The van's first run would be short and sweet. A little close to home perhaps, but there were just so many tightly-packed Gatsos in the East Midlands.

The police in Harlow were busy that Sunday. Some grumbled about ma'am wanting them in on a Sunday; others were pleased to pocket the overtime pay.

Two computers stored still images, a third showed a video – taken using a powerful zoom lens from a well-hidden location in the Princess Royal Stand.

The SCT files already held images of Gavin, Sue and J.J., since his Boat Race appearance. The legality of the images was dubious.

They soon had fixes on McIvor and Proust as plain-clothes cops had relayed information on their accents and checked the names with a friendly hotel receptionist.

"So, that's our famous five," said ACC Hayes to the room. "Could any of this lot be our man? Who's checking them out?"

DS Alex Scott replied: "Waiting for Dundee to wake up, ma'am, but so far all I've got on the jock are a couple of motoring offences."

"Nothing yet on the big bugger," said DS Wickford. "Looks the type to have a record, doesn't he? I'm hoping for a call back within the hour. Keep you posted, ma'am."

"What about their loony assistants? Any fix on them?"

"We're checking number plates, ma'am," said DC Granier. "But from their photos I can't say any of them stand out as the vandal-type."

"And we've definitely ruled out our blond friend?"

"Yes, ma'am," said DS Pierce. "Seems he rarely leaves Essex, must have had a visa go to north."

Humour was thin on the ground at the SCT.

"Right, keep checking everyone."

DS Wickford received his call on time. His contact in the intelligence service had some information on the big bugger. He had phoned

James Rolands at MI5 when Leeds police reported that they had little on Proust, though he did have a military file outside their jurisdiction. Did the Harlow sergeant want them to get clearance from on high? No, he would handle it himself, thanks.

After speaking with Rolands, DS Wickford took a deep breath and went to see his boss.

"Our Neil Proust is a former military man, ma'am – Royal Marines and, more famously, the Special Boat Service. He's been around. Decorated in the first Gulf War, spent some time in Washington on a joint effort with American anti-terrorism units. My contact says there was a red file that he could not access without getting a password from his superior. That usually means something murky in Northern Ireland, from his experience.

"Proust was honourably discharged two years ago. Now drives a truck for a firm in Leeds. Married, one grown-up kid. No criminal record, not even a motoring offence. Leeds police have no idea why he is mixed up with this SCATE mob."

ACC Hayes thought for a moment before asking her sergeant: "Does he ride a motorbike?"

DS Wickford tried not to blush. The motorbike was his angle and had drawn one big blank. "I'll check that out, ma'am."

"Good, please do. From the five we know of, this chap looks our most likely candidate. He'd have the expertise to pull off something like this. Shame he's a bloody war hero. He'll simply have to learn that even our Special Forces have to live within the law.

"See if we can make a discreet check with his employer to find out his whereabouts on the nights in question. But I don't want anyone to alert him to our interest. Get the Leeds boys to create a fictitious accident involving a truck similar to his. You know the routine."

Mixed news drifted onto DS Wickford's desk throughout the day. The Driver and Vehicle Licensing Agency in Swansea did indeed have a motorcycle registered to Neil Proust. What neither the DVLA nor DS Wickford could know, however, was that the Triumph 400 had not left Proust's garage for eight months.

Fred Harrison was not pleased when the two Leeds officers disturbed his Sunday TV viewing. But the haulage boss obliged and checked his logs. Yes, two of his drivers were out that night. Neil Proust was returning from Harwich and Greg Yates was down in Cornwall. The officers apologised for interrupting the big game, thanked Fred for his assistance and they were happy to rule his trucks out of their enquiries.

The SCT team assembled for a final briefing before the benevolent ACC Hayes allowed them back to their families for what remained of that Sunday.

DS Wickford was just off the phone with the Leeds detectives. He informed his colleagues of his news.

"So now we know Mr Proust was on the road on the night of the attacks in Scotland," said ACC Hayes. "But he was down here – allegedly – not over the border. What do we make of that?"

"Assuming this is our man, perhaps he arranged for someone else to drive the truck for him?" suggested DC Granier.

"He did foreign runs and would need a passport. Sounds too elaborate," said DS Wickford.

DS Sarah Williams felt the time was right to test her theory. "I was wondering whether we could be looking for more than one bloke, ma'am? Makes sense looking at the amount of ground covered."

"The planning certainly has a military feel to it," said DS Pierce. "A group of pissed off vets?"

"Let's keep all options open. I'd like this Proust watched for a few days. By our own officers, not the local lads. Wickford and Pierce, you look like you could do with some Yorkshire air in your lungs. Pack your bags for Leeds in the morning, and not a word to the locals.

"Remember, this chap is highly trained and potentially dangerous. Don't get too close, and back off if he clocks you. Don't forget, also, that until proven otherwise he is a highly-respected pillar of society.

"The rest of us will reconvene here in the morning and continue the checks until we get a positive ID from Wickford and Pierce. We still work on the assumption that our man could be anyone. I want no mention that Proust is a possible culprit outside these walls. Thank you for your attendance this fine Sunday."

ACC Hayes was surprised by her thoughts on the road home. She had suspected SCATE were behind the vandalism. Now she wasn't sure. But just maybe this Proust was operating without the collusion of the others. They had seemed an innocent bunch of idiots at the races.

Let's see what my boys dig up in Leeds, she sighed.

CHAPTER ELEVEN

Enter The Trilby

There is an unofficial network of Special Forces vets whose arms reach across many friendly nations. It has no formal structure. Its members require no discipline. They exist to help each other, inside or outside the law.

They help colleagues in trouble, in debt, or who have fallen on hard times. Neil Proust had served alongside many of the British members. He had once been called upon to help an old soldier in the network, or rather the soldier's wife.

She had almost lost her life due to a drug overdose. Proust and another vet ensured her supply of heroin in Bradford dried up by paying the dealer a visit. They had wanted to kill him, but one of the network's unofficial rules was 'kill only when there is no alternative.' This unofficial rule allows some of the dregs of society to still roam the streets.

Proust was scheduled to leave on another long haul to northern Europe on the Wednesday. A brief phone chat and Davie McAllister arranged to meet him at the Leicester Forest East service station on the M1.

Proust noticed nothing unusual on the Monday as he walked his dog, took his wife shopping and enjoyed a few pints down the local.

He became aware he was being watched at lunchtime on the Tuesday as he went to post a letter. That red Cavalier was driving ever so slowly, and he was sure he had seen it before but couldn't pinpoint where. His suspicions were confirmed early evening as he drove his wife to a local restaurant – their usual haunt before he hit the road. Later that night he told his beloved Mrs Irene Proust that he fancied some fresh air before bed. He checked for snoopers as he walked the streets. Convinced he was alone, he dived into the public phone booth and rang Davie McAllister.

He didn't want to arouse suspicion by letting his watchers see him there so he quickly informed McAllister. They would stick to their rendez-vous but not acknowledge each other's existence. There was no sign of the red Cavalier as he walked home.

The red Cavalier had been parked up for the night and sergeants Wickford and Pierce were sampling the local brews. They had called it a night when Proust and his wife returned home from the restaurant just before 10pm.

Two days of discreet surveillance had revealed nothing untoward, they had informed ACC Hayes. They were to stick with their man on his journey to Harwich the next day and report back to Harlow on Thursday.

They did as ordered. They saw nothing unusual as an old man in a trilby hat sat three seats away from Proust at the service station and nibbled at a roast dinner. They left the diner a minute after Proust and did not see the man swiftly pocket a sheaf of papers from underneath Proust's plate.

The man in the trilby wasn't as old as he had made himself appear. Fifty-one years old Davie McAllister was a seasoned Special Air Service campaigner. He had worked undercover in Ulster, served in the Falklands and fought in many more skirmishes around the globe.

He drove to his Nottingham home and studied the papers with fellow SAS veteran Colin Jefferson.

Proust had left a note explaining why he wanted Dr Glue warning off. He also left details on the Allinns uncovered by Gavin and Sue. The former SAS warriors decided to start the job first thing in the morning. The 43-year-old Jefferson lost the toss and would be the driver.

Allinn's ride out in his new van on Tuesday night proved more thrilling than he had assumed. He was sure the bike had to stay behind and he would need a new style of vandalism; the police had begun alarming Gatsos, particularly the replacement ones, and there had been stories in the Press concerning rapid response squads on the look-out for wreckers. This was more wishful thinking on behalf of the transport department than a reality.

Allinn had made notes on two-dozen Gatsos on a short route, using the A6 and the A46 between Leicester and Nottingham.

The tool bag he filled and placed in the back of the van was much heavier than usual as he had borrowed an industrial metal-cutter from a local builder. The glue was sadly missing – replaced by a small tube of regular super-glue, damned expensive for such a small amount. There would be ample for what Allinn required that night.

He drove off and was soon approaching his chosen ones. The first Gatso was ideally situated but a clear warning sign that it was alarmed disturbed the wrecker. He decided then that he would like to risk an alarmed one as his final job for the night.

Eight miles later he was pleased he had avoided it when a much better choice sprang into view. The Gatso was hidden behind a large sycamore tree, but there was no cover to the nearside. A lay-by was less than a hundred yards away so there would be no great sweat lugging his heavy equipment.

He donned his overalls and approached the Gatso. He sported a flu-

-orescent hard hat on top of his curly wig. The job took him less than a minute.

He had practised with the power saw in his garage and was pleased it cut through the metal surround of the speed camera's column base. He had been careful not to damage any of the internal wiring. He puffed and grunted as he twisted the whole column ninety degrees to his left and then stuck a card over the manufacturer's logo – the Son of Dr Glue hoped they enjoyed the new view.

The camera was still operational, but it would not be trapping speeding motorists for a while. The lens was facing a small open field. By morning, Allinn wondered if a few cows might be grazing. He hoped they'd obey the 50mph limit and not trigger the camera.

A handful of vehicles had zipped by while Allinn was at work, but none had seemed to pay him any notice.

He was satisfied with another job well done but realised his heart was thumping as he settled in his van and drove off. He had spent much longer on the job than on previous outings; he had been more visible. A new buzz brightened his journey.

He abandoned one target when a police car whizzed past just as he was parking up.

He was surprised by the sudden appearance of some students out for a midnight jog as he was leaving the site of his third job near Loughborough. Allinn had been delayed there when his saw almost ripped through a wire inside the Gatso column but he delicately prised it free from the teeth of the blade. He assured himself the joggers hadn't seen him and pressed on.

The only time he really missed the Yamaha was close to Nottingham when he feared he was being followed. A few nervous miles followed during which he spent more time checking his rear view mirror than watching the road and seeking good targets. His bike would have lost the headlights of the dark saloon car within seconds, he growled.

Convinced it was a false alarm after he had made a minor detour, Allinn retraced his route to tackle one of the most-profitable speed cameras in the Midlands. One bank holiday weekend the previous summer it had raked in more than £1 million in fines.

Not surprisingly, Allinn found it had an alarm fitted. He paid it due respect and was extra careful, even making a trial cut before slicing through the inch thick metal casing. He twisted this one round to the right so that its lens was fixed on a row of commercial units 150 yards away. His card was placed over the alarm warning. Allinn completed his missions and was home by 2am, satisfied with his new gimmick.

He could have managed more but settled for five that night. It had been warm in the van, and the radio chat show had been amusing company, even if some of the callers needed their heads examined.

A news item grabbed his attention; four drivers in the British Rally had been found guilty that day and handed fines and penalty points each.

Three unfortunate foreign rally stars had been flashed several times which automatically took them over the 12-point mark. They would not be spending their summer vacations in Britain after being banned from driving on her roads for six months.

Organisers were raging and claimed Britain's status as a leading rally venue was under threat. The item ended with the solemn announcement that the number of motorists trapped by speed cameras that year was approaching a staggering FOUR million. Allinn was pleased that the good, old BBC had branded them speed not safety cameras. He and Gavin Lloyd had that in common.

Eighteen hours passed before the first damaged Gatso was detected. The calling card alerted the officers who passed on the bad news to Harlow.

His colleagues had gone for the night when DC Tony Granier took the call. He sat for a few minutes and wondered what action to take. His SCT colleagues had little to report to him as he started his shift; no new leads and thankfully no fresh vandalism. Should he inform ACC Hayes? Or perhaps DS Wickford first?

He rang the Nottinghamshire officers and kindly suggested they check the other cameras in the vicinity to see if they were operating normally as this guy usually wrecked bunches at a time.

Four hours later, he was told five in total had been damaged – all with the same MO. Although there had been no wanton smashing of the camera equipment, the Gatsos would require specialist attention as the metal casings were beyond repair. Cards were found at each location, but, sorry, it would be morning before any forensic evidence could be checked out.

DC Granier felt like telling the officers not to waste their time on forensics but understood they had to follow the routine.

It was approaching two in the morning. He persuaded himself little was to be gained by phoning the chief now; she needed her beauty sleep more than most. He determined to phone her at 6am so she would at least be able to digest the news on her way to the HQ.

He would make certain there was a detailed report on her desk. He rang Nottingham again and requested scans of the calling cards, exact locations and precise times of the last vehicles flashed by each camera. It felt good issuing instructions to officers often senior in rank.

"Why didn't you inform me sooner?" snapped ACC Hayes when

Granier disturbed her shower.

"The local boys were still collecting evidence, ma'am. I have a full report ready for you, though they are still awaiting forensics."

"Be there in 50 minutes. Tell Wickford and the others I want them in smartish, too."

DS Sarah Williams was the last to arrive, a few minutes before 8am after hastily dumping her children with an understanding neighbour.

"So it appears our man really did run out of glue," ACC Hayes told her team. "Still, I want that angle kept in play. You never know."

"You can rule out our war hero, ma'am," said DS Wickford. "He was home with his wife on Tuesday night. We followed him yesterday and watched him check his lorry onto the ferry."

"I've just had time to glance through Tony's report ma'am. But it says no cameras were damaged, just the outsides. You think the alarms scared him off smashing them up?" said DS Pierce.

"Only one of 'em was alarmed, according to the locals," informed Granier.

"Let's assume just another of his little games," said ACC Hayes. "It seems obvious he enjoys his private jokes...and his card games. Let's have another look at the geography, shall we."

ACC Hayes walked over to a huge wall map. Coloured pins marked the scenes of their villain's crimes. She drew a circle with her pen around a vast area of England.

"Let's forget Scotland for now, and all furthest points north, south, east and west. Would I be too far out of it to suggest our man either lives in this central area – or at least spends a considerable amount of his time there?"

There was silence while the officers let her comments sink in. DS

Wickford was first to reply:

"Makes sense, ma'am. I can't think of any other reason why he would chose the East Mids so soon after hitting East Anglia."

"Nor me. And let us not forget his little excursion to my home. A great, great pity I wasn't at home to receive him. So, let's concentrate our minds on this area south of Nottingham, shall we," ACC Hayes often added 'shall we' to her comments. She always made it sound like an instruction rather than query. "What do we make of that, then?" This time it was a question.

"Three of his five outings have ended in this area," DS Alex Scott now drew an imaginary circle around a section of the map. "Four, errm, if we include the visit to your house, ma'am."

"Good. Maybe, just a little maybe for now, we are getting somewhere. Until we hear otherwise let's narrow down our search. We have just ruled out from our enquiries around 20 million British motorists. I do feel so much better. But let's not get carried away. What about age?"

"I'd say young, ma'am. Late 20s at most," said DC Granier. "Reasonably strong, too, judging by last night's effort. Can't be easy twisting those buggers round."

"I wouldn't argue with you constable. But let's raise the profile a few notches before we go off chasing a budding Arnold Schwarzenegger. For now, make it a man under 45, some of our citizens do manage to keep in shape despite the rage in junk food, don't they boys?" A rare smile from the chief.

"I think last night disproved the motorcycle theory, ma'am," said DS Wickford. "Sorry, I know it was my theory but I can't see a vandal carrying a chain-saw around on his back."

"Any word on the make of saw he used, Granier?"

"Not yet, ma'am. I did ask the locals last night when one of them told me the camera had been sliced clean through, neat work it was, he said."

"Hurry them up. Might give us an important lead if it is a specialist tool. We need to know if there is any link between the glue and this new method."

"If any outlets distribute both items we may have something, ma'am," said DS Wickford.

"Right, action then. DS Wickford can check out the tools used last night. DS Williams, compile a dossier of all the glue outlets inside that area.

"And I think it's time to ask the friendly public again. DS Scott, liaise with the locals and arrange for some signboards at the latest locations. Stress that I insist all of them are covered. They should be freshest in a few memories, hopefully.

"Finally, nothing to the Press. Not that I should need to mention that." She put on her stern face. "Please ask Nottingham to pass all Press enquiries through here. I will draft a short note for the media office now. Not a word to any of your friendly hacks, OK."

DS Pierce clapped his arm round DS Wickford as the officers went to their respective tasks.

"My money was on the motorbike, if it's any consolation, Steve. I had this mental image of a crazed Hell's Angel who had cameras tattooed all over his chest. He was foaming at the mouth as six of us wrestled him to the ground."

"Fuck off, smart-arse." But Wickford was seasoned enough to share the laughter with his colleague. Both wanted to get back to chasing real Essex villains. It wasn't as if they were in short supply.

ACC Hayes swiftly provided the media office with a blunt statement.

Dr Glue was responsible for more vandalism, they believed. They were working on several new leads and would keep the Press updated. If any member of the public had any information, which could help the police catch this man who was endangering lives on the roads, they could call the special police hotline.

The SCT chief then wrote a brief summary of the night's events for the transport secretary. She thought it was best if the news came from her.

Her report ruined a promising Thursday for Sean Chapman. He had been jauntier these last few days as Dr Glue's silence gave transport policy a welcome respite in the national media.

His life hadn't been Gatso-free as his department daily dispatched bulletins updating the so-called successes of their policy. Responses, allegedly from the transport secretary, were forwarded to whichever specialist motoring magazines required them.

The Home Secretary deftly fielded one question about the police hunt for Britain's most notorious vandal, but largely the public – or their media representatives – seemed more concerned with foreign policy and the worrying increase in asylum seekers.

"The bastard's back!" snarled Chapman as he stomped around his spacious office, clenching and unclenching his fists. No matter what his mood, he could never look menacing.

"I can't believe it. We've given the police every resource they've asked for and they haven't a bloody clue where to look for this bastard. They've narrowed down their search, she says. South and East of England indeed – just 20-odd million people to interview then. She must think I'm bloody stupid.

"You'd better prepare a Press Release, Simon. I should just go and try and grab the PM's attention for a few of his precious moments.

Don't want the lobby chaps springing anything on him. That wouldn't do at all."

"What would you like me to say to the Press this time, sir? Do I release it immediately?"

"No, don't let it out yet. Wait until someone asks for statement. Just rattle off the usual...we have every confidence that the police will be successful in apprehending and bringing to justice this lout blah blah...you know the drill."

CHAPTER TWELVE

Albert's Lovely Mother

Chapman escaped that Thursday. The Press release was sent out following request for a Government response, but to the transport secretary's relief the national tabloids on Friday were more concerned with who was groping whom at one of the ever-increasing number of awards ceremonies.

Speed cameras were indeed relegated to low-profile when The Guardian had an exclusive story that Prime Minister Laurence Carr was planning a snap election the following month.

He would go to the public primarily on a question of confidence in his Government's handling of the European issue, a high-up inside source had leaked to The Guardian.

The ruling Labour Party still had a year of its term to run, but PM Carr hoped to strike while the polls were still slightly in his favour. Two referendums on Europe had failed to quell sniping from several quarters.

Caroline Mitchell was delighted by the news. Naturally, she would not expect confirmation of the story until the PM was ready to announce Election Day. But she would put money on it being true.

She thought Carr was being foolish to try and con the British public that a domestic election could be run on a single issue, a foreign one at that. Typical of his self-righteous attitude; he shakes hands with a few foreign leaders and gets all high and mighty.

The usual issues that concerned the British electorate would win the day: the economy, health and education.

Foreign issues would obviously hold sway with some, as would a variety of relatively lesser issues. Mitchell would sweat blood to ensure that transport – and, more particularly, transport policing – was as high on the agenda as possible.

A recent survey had revealed that nine per cent of the British public had little confidence in the Government's transport policies. Not a great percentage, but compared to the one per cent who claimed to have every confidence in this Government on transport it revealed to Mitchell that many thousands of votes were up for grabs on this topic.

They could swing the vote the Tories' way, and in due course advance her career a few rungs. Mitchell had no plan or desire to be stuck in transport for the rest of her political life.

Yes, let the big boys debate the under-funding of schools, the lack of hospital beds, the housing crisis, the influx of asylum seekers and even bloody Europe. She would nibble away at the edges of the electorate and ensure that Samuel Owens realised what a wonderful asset he had fighting by his side.

The scheming side of her wanted to kiss Dr Glue.

Davie McAllister had little concern with politics. He had been sent into battle – officially and unofficially – by governments of both colours.

He didn't really care too much about speed cameras, either. But for a fellow vet like Neil Proust there was little that he would not do. And once Proust had revealed his reasons for joining SCATE and the tragic circumstances of his comrade's death, McAllister vowed to get this lout dealt with promptly and efficiently.

So while Ms Mitchell and her Westminster chums were preparing their troops for their battle, McAllister was that same morning on the trail of Dr Glue.

SCATE

He was annoying his driver by firing crossword questions at him as they waited outside the Wolverhampton home of Mr Kevin Allinn. Their man lived in a three-bed semi-detached two miles from the city centre. The lawn had been mown recently and the front garden possessed a few clumps of spring flowers.

They hadn't wanted to involve any of their other helpers, and as it was a short drive from their Nottinghamshire homes they would check him out themselves.

If McAllister had not been such a remarkable character – almost a father figure to him – Colin Jefferson would have knocked his trilby flying and let him know he preferred flying bullets to flying, bloody-stupid, who-gives-a-toss crossword questions.

Thankfully, they had not waited long when a shortish man left the front door of the house. Quick as a flash, McAllister was out of the car and approaching the garden gate. He was all smiles.

"Good morning, sir. I'm looking for a Mr Kevin Allinn. Is this the right address?"

"That's me. What can I do for you?" The man had clearly been retired a few years.

McAllister looked puzzled. "I'm from the insurance company, sir? You requested a personal visit for a quote on a Lotus?"

"A Lotus? Me?" the pensioner chuckled.

McAllister appeared to share the amusement. "Don't suppose you have a son, sir?"

"No, laddie. Just our Janet. She could probably afford a Lotus these days. But she's living in Sydney."

"Looks like someone's pulling our legs, sir. Apologies for the inconvenience." McAllister tipped his hat one more time and went back to join Jefferson.

"Typical. I told you we should have tried the closest one first. Drive on, old chap."

The traffic was a pain even outside rush-hour. McAllister had given up on the crossword and the two vets chatted about old times and old soldiers. Jefferson was happier.

There was no parking space by the next Kevin Allinn's flat, so they had to leave their vehicle 700 yards away on a supermarket car park and approach on foot up a steep hill.

They did a recce of the flat and discovered no-one at home. Jefferson managed to glance inside the flat as he waited in vain for someone to answer the bell.

"Looks like the guy lives alone," he told McAllister.

McAllister stopped a passer-by. "Sorry, madam," he tipped his trilby and pointed to the flat. "Do you know Kevin? We expected him in this afternoon."

"Usually is around this time. Only works weekends. You can check if his bike's in the garage."

With that the woman pushed on with her pushchair and was out of earshot as the ever-so polite vet thanked her.

The vets cleared the grime from the garage window and peered inside. It was a tight squeeze but the garage could just about hold the Yamaha Muscle and the Peugeot van. He probably hadn't gone far then.

"Looks like this is the one we want," said Jefferson. "I'll let you apologise if we're wrong. You're better at it than me."

They walked to a nearby park and sat on a bench which afforded a clear view of Allinn's flat. They'd give it two hours and return later if he hadn't shown.

Jefferson alleviated his boredom by messing around on the swings;

he was never the greatest of watchers.

They were almost ready to hunt down a suitable hostelry for a late lunch when a figure tottered up the lane and began prodding at the keyhole to Allinn's flat. The figure eventually managed to negotiate his key into the hole and let himself into the flat.

"Fond of a few lunchtime pints, myself," sniggered Jefferson. "Do we go in now or let him sleep it off?"

"Let's give him a couple of hours to get cosy. He's made me all thirsty. Shame you're driving."

Allinn was fast asleep as Jefferson and McAllister entered his flat. They owned keys for each and every occasion. They were as light on their feet as ballet dancers.

No words were needed between them. McAllister clamped his strong tape over the sleeping vandal's mouth, and by the time the wide-eyed Allinn had attempted unsuccessfully to raise from his bed, Jefferson had his hands firmly tied with heavy-duty rope.

They gave him a few seconds to get accustomed to their smiling faces.

"Dr Glue, I presume," McAllister tipped his hat. "Don't worry, we're not with the police. We just want a little chat. Just nod your head when you're ready to co-operate and I'll remove the tape. I should say that you'd be foolish to disappoint me."

Jefferson was walking around the flat, examining Allinn's CD collection, his books, his wardrobe. He powered up the computer and connected to the Internet. The former SAS man smiled and turned to the bed as scate.co.uk came into view.

"Unusual choice for a homepage, isn't it?"

Allinn was clearly scared rigid. Sweat had started pouring from his forehead and was dripping onto his pillow. He wanted to nod his head but his muscles would not obey his brain.

Both men left the bedside and continued browsing through his belongings. Jefferson showed McAllister a pile of books and documents which he had picked up from underneath a desk.

There were maps and printed pages listing Gatsos across the UK. A thick scrapbook was entertaining McAllister.

"Proud of your exploits, aren't you? A regular soldier. Fancy a chat yet?"

At last Allinn managed to co-ordinate his functions and gave a slight nod.

"You sure?"

Allinn nodded again, more vigourously.

McAllister ripped away the tape. Allinn bolted up in his bed and rubbed his mouth.

"Who are you? What do you want?" he gasped.

"A friendly chat, that's all. There's absolutely no need to involve the police. Unless you want to, of course?"

Jefferson handed Allinn a glass of water. "Here, drink this, it'll make you feel better."

He sat down on the opposite side of the bed. Both men smiled at the scared stiff Allinn. No matter how hard they tried, their smiles could not appear friendly.

"Why don't you start at the very beginning? That's a very good place to start," a sing-song tone in Jefferson's voice.

It took a few more minutes for Allinn to settle his nerves, a few more frightened queries: "Who are you? What do you want?"

He had little option but to trust the pair. If they weren't cops and about to nick him what harm could come to him?

His glass was refilled and his mind as fresh as it could be in the cir-

-cumstances as he began to pour out his story – from the very beginning, starting with the offence which almost cost him his job.

The two men made the occasional sympathetic noise but did nothing to interrupt Allinn's amusing narrative.

Ten minutes later, Allinn flicked his eyes from man to man. "That's it. What are you going to do to me?"

McAllister clapped his hands together and got up from the bed.

"What a truly wonderful story. You have a gift."

He sat down again and assumed his best bedside manner. He stared intently into Allinn's eyes. "I can't recall the last time one anyone told me a fairytale. The most amazing thing is, Kevin, I actually believe every word of it. Every word. Now, does this fairytale have a happy ending? They usually do."

"There's usually a moral to a fairy story. That's what my old mum always told me," said Jefferson. "The hero had to learn his lesson, right?"

McAllister got up and clapped his hands again. He pointed at Jefferson and exclaimed: "That's it, Albert! Your old mum was a gem. She should have been a judge. So, Kevin, here's what we do."

Allinn tried to remain alert in his confusion. There was something very strange about these guys, something weirdly comic, and something at the same time weirdly frightening.

Jefferson untied his hands and both men gave him hearty slaps on the back.

"Bet you feel a whole lot better now that's off your chest, eh? We're trusting you, so you can trust us. Nothing silly now and we can all be friends."

The grip McAllister had on his shoulder told Allinn it would be wise to keep on the friendly side of this strange bloke and his sidekick.

Allinn told them he had operated alone and no other person was aware of his identity. He was puzzled how they had discovered him. "A friend," was all they would reveal.

"But the cops would have been here soon, Kevin, if we hadn't arrived to rescue you from...what? Two years at least for the damage you have done. Ever been inside? Not much fun from what some bad, bad men have told me."

They ran through their list of instructions. It was up to Allinn whether he carried them out, as his neck was on the line, not theirs.

He would hand over to them any papers which could link him to Dr Glue. He would have to clean his computer himself; that was really not their scene. If the police did call, he would have to do his best to ward them off. Pity he had no friend to provide alibis. He could possibly get away just being out for a spin on his bike, but he would need a half-decent excuse to explain away the van ride. Maybe a casual girl pick-up.

Just so he didn't have any second thoughts, they would be 'borrowing' his motorcycle. Jefferson was flicking through his key ring and prised two free. He would get it back for good behaviour.

"Best of luck," said Jefferson as they made to leave.

"One last thing," McAllister turned and gave him that smile again. He whispered something out of Jefferson's earshot. Allinn gave the vet an even more puzzled look but nodded as if in agreement.

A weird, weird pair, thought the now-retired Public Vandal Number One as he started undressing. He desperately hoped a good shower would wash away the memory of a very strange and frightening visit.

Jefferson rode the Yamaha down to the supermarket car park. He had seen a dirt track running by the huge store. He guided the bike gently over a flowerbed and found a suitable spot a few yards into some trees. He went into the store and bought some heavy plastic sheeting.

He returned to the bike and put on a pair of gloves. He unwrapped the sheeting and carefully made sure it covered the whole bike. He covered the plastic with branches and twigs. Once satisfied it would be unnoticeable to a casual stroller, he returned to the car just in time to see the trilby bobbing along.

Happy with their work – not a great ordeal in the scheme of their hazardous lives – the men drove home.

"Albert? Albert? Where the hell did that name come from?" asked Jefferson.

"Not sure," laughed McAllister loudly. "But I'm told he had a lovely mother."

Terry Chapman was slightly miffed by the news that his weekend driver would not have his motorcycle available for a while. The van would slow him down but, honest boss, I'll get all the jobs done.

He was returning from a drop-off in the Peak District on Sunday when he pulled into an Internet café in Buxton. Dr Glue made his final post:

Dear Friends,
I have decided to retire from my practice. I am sorry for any incon-venience I may have caused. I now know that peaceful protest is the key to success. I would especially like to thank Albert's mum for making me see the light.
Drive safely
Love Dr Glue

The SCT was disbanded three weeks after Allinn's last post. There was no need for it any longer. They had failed to catch Public Vandal Number One and now it really did seem as though he had ceased his wrecking sprees.

A few so-called Friends Of Dr Glue had been arrested at various locations in England and Wales. Interrogations proved no link with their infamous mentor.

Sporadic damage continued, but that was a job for local police. ACC Hayes had failed in her first nationwide role.

She was angry and confused. Who on earth was he? Where did he live? Was she sure it was just one bloke? Did he ride a motorcycle? Why had he quit so suddenly? The questions haunted her for months as she returned to routine deskwork.

Less than a week later, Laurence Carr informed the nation that he was going to the polls to seek public support for his Government's decision to strengthen political links with her European colleagues. He had decided against another referendum after much deliberation. His Cabinet was united – closer ties with Europe were the way ahead. Vote Labour for a brighter future at the heart of the continent.

DS Wickford went back to grabbing a variety of bad 'uns. On the day of PM Carr's announcement, he decided to pay Gavin Lloyd a courtesy call. He was on his way back from an interview in Frowstone when he arrived at the Lloyd household early one Friday evening.

Sue answered the door.

"Hello, is Gavin in? Don't worry it's not an official visit."

Gavin appeared. "Sergeant Wickford? What can we do for you?"

"I was just passing by and thought I'd call. Looks like you have a party going on. Sorry to interrupt but I thought you might like this back...as a memento. We don't need it any longer."

SCATE

The officer handed Gavin the card Dr Glue had posted through his letterbox.

"Great. Thanks. Why don't you join us for a drink?"

"Thanks. Just a coffee, though, please."

It wasn't really a party, but the atmosphere inside the Lloyd household was jovial and occasionally raucous.

The police officer was introduced to Gavin's children and Sue for the first time. Kate was swigging some hideously-coloured alcopop and Jim having the time of his life sharing cans of Australian lager with the adults.

All the SCATE members were in attendance. Neil Proust had brought along his long-time friend Davie McAllister. Of course, Davie's involvement in their mystery was destined to remain a secret, even to the other SCATE members.

Guest of honour was Pete Hampson. He was enjoying his liberty and looking forward to relaunching his business career. He'd had a few pints with Gavin at the 'Dog' and was now guzzling red wine like there was no tomorrow.

Gavin made sure all the guests were quickly aware that their new friend had been a member of the SCT. Steve Wickford was happy to relate a few stories from their fruitless search for Dr Glue, and he took the light-hearted ribbing in good heart.

After a while, he wandered out onto the patio for a smoke. Frank McIvor and McAllister were engaged in an excited discussion about the relative merits of various malt whiskies.

Something stirred inside the copper as the trilby was tipped in his direction. The trilby puzzled him as he drove home to Chelmsford. Why did the hat look familiar but not the guy?

By Saturday morning it was a distant memory.

EPILOGUE

The Power Of The Pen

Gavin was sweating before he got to the polling station, even though it was just a short walk from his home.

By the time he was in the booth, his shirt was soaked.

His pen hovered over the paper. Could he really forsake 36 years of socialist upbringing?

His pen seemed to hover for an eternity before it swooped and a crisp X was placed in the box alongside the name of Humphrey Bellow.

Sorry Fred 'The Red' Simmons.

Gavin had the glint of contentment in his eyes. Yes, Humphrey Bellow and Samuel Owens and Caroline Mitchell were the ones for him; the ones to make good on their promises.

Suddenly, Gavin's air changed from one of satisfaction. His eyes became glazed and fixed on some indeterminate spot on the flimsy piece of paper that carried such weight and power.

He dived into his pocket and plucked out his trusty red felt-tipped pen. And, sporting one of the broadest smiles ever seen inside a British polling booth, he scrawled diagonally across the paper:

Special thanks to Karla Mahar for editorial assistance and to Tom Butterworth for his technical expertise and occasional patience.

www.tomjsandy.co.uk   www.scate.co.uk

TOM J SANDY

Tom J Sandy was born in Bury,
Lancashire and graduated in history
from the University of North
Humberside, Hull. He lives in
Essex, with his two children.
He is the author of **Perverting The
Course Of Justice**, which is to be
published by **Eye 5** in 2005.
Sandy is currently finishing a third
book.

AUTHOR'S NOTE

I was first Gatso'd early one morning on a deserted M11.
Only one camera in ten has film in it, a friend informed
me. I didn't learn the lesson, as they say, until a ban
came along. Now my children accuse me of driving my
battered but still trusty Ford Mondeo too slowly.

So, yes, I suppose Gavin Lloyd is loosely based on my
own experiences at the hands of the faceless speed cameras.

Many years ago I owned a motorcycle, but nothing as
grand as Kevin Allinn's Yamaha. I fell off, got back on
just to prove I had no fear...and saved for a car.

Since moving to Essex 16 years ago I have driven more
than a quarter of a million miles. I have been stopped a
couple of times during Christmas drink-drive blitzes,
passing safely, obviously. I have been stopped twice at
ungodly hours by polite Essex officers, pointing out problems with rear lights. Get it sorted first thing in the
morning, OK sir?

If you are stopped by a police officer, be courteous. If
you get flashed by a speed camera, you may rant.

Drive safely.

Tom J Sandy

Also by TOM J SANDY

Perverting The Course Of Justice

Stunning libel thriller with a savage
sting in the tail.

A senior detective is accused of being involved
with a ring of child pornographers.

Can Britain's most flamboyant barrister
clear his name?

Published by Eye 5 - 2005

Perverting The Course Of Justice

(Eye 5 - published 2005)

EXTRACT FROM CHAPTER ONE

No-one had overheard Terry James's phone conversation. Afterwards, he had gone immediately to Editor Andrew Harvey's office and entered without even bothering to knock.

"Just had a call from a contact, boss. A big one – Henry Headleigh's involved in some kiddie ring. Thought I should come and see you first."

"Involved? Involved? Of course, he's bloody involved; he's in charge of it. What are you trying to tell me, young man?"

Harvey was a craggy Scot who had joined so many of his race in acquiring a seat of considerable power at the high table of British journalism. The 47-year-old had quit his job as news editor at a national broadsheet paper to assume editorship of the Gazette three years ago.

His hard-nose for news rather than the waffly, ubiquitous women's features had sparked a steady rise in the Gazette's circulation and earned Harvey a very lucrative annual bonus.

The accountants regretted the proprietor's decision to heavily weigh Harvey's salary on bonuses. Thankfully, former porn king Bryan Richardson did occasionally ignore the moneymen. He was happy to hand over a 78-85k annual bonus to Harvey, especially as advertising revenue grew in line with circulation.

The Gazette regularly scooped the nationals on the big London stories, even those papers with more money to chuck around than commonsense.

Naturally, Harvey was canny enough to know his many affluent readers wanted to know what to wear at their smart Chelsea eateries (why didn't his reporters call them restaurants these days?), and what was hot and what was not (in the pop charts, at the cinema, in holiday destinations, in clothes, in table chat).

Those issues bored Harvey rigid but he was decent enough to let his middle-ranking executives have their way. Most of the time.

But give him a good old-fashioned hard news story and Harvey was like a dog gnawing on a bone; he would refuse to let go until he was satisfied he had ripped away all the flesh. In truth, Harvey would gnaw away at a story more than any sensible dog would at a bone.

"Pray enlighten me. Is this some new involvement I am not aware of? Are you going to tell me our police hero is one of the sickos?" Harvey turned away from his computer screen and gave James his undivided attention.

"That's exactly it, boss. Just had a call from a source. He told me Headleigh has been seeing some paedos across the water in Kent, and it wasn't undercover work either. He gave me three dates when Headleigh attended private functions at the house of one of this group."

"Hang on a minute, Terry. You're telling me Detective Superintendent Henry Headleigh is indulging in the sick fantasies of this group? You're telling me Henry Headleigh is a bloody paedophile?"

"Hard to believe, I know. But, yes, it seems Headleigh has a liking for young East European girls. The Kent group has first bite at them it appears, before they are shipped off to the big cities. Of course, they're all illegals. They arrive through Dover, Folkestone and the Channel Tunnel. One of the group also has some private landing spot by Whitstable, I am told."

"Bloody hell! And you're certain this is kosher?"

"Absolutely, boss. Comes from a solid contact. I've used him before and he's never let me down. He gave me the gangland murder stuff last year. He kept me one step ahead of the herd, remember? And he tipped me off about the drugs killings – Harry Nickels and his mob in Basildon."

Harvey certainly did remember several of the many Terry James exclusives. He shouted through to his secretary in the annexe: "Give Arthur Jacobs a buzz, Irene. Tell him to make himself available down here in ten minutes."

He turned back to face James. "OK, Terry. Run the facts by me. Slowly."

"Well my source tells me Kent police have been keeping an eye on Headleigh for some time. They have kept it within their own paedo unit but I am told it's going to break this weekend. A raid is planned on the ring-leader's home in Chatham.

"They have seen Headleigh visit this guy's house on three occasions. He's also been spotted at parties held at two other houses in the Maidstone area. Seems he is at least discreet enough to operate outside his own patch.

"They've also found a credit card used to access sick websites. It belongs to Headleigh and they believe he uses his personal computer to access them, and not one of Essex Police's. That figures as the cops are under instructions to use only special police cards for investigating this kind of thing; to protect themselves mainly. He's known to have been in email contact with two of the group."

"Christ! This is hard to believe – Mr Squeaky Clean, Scourge of the Essex Mafia. Kids of his own, hasn't he?"

"Yes, three grown-up now."

"Happily married?"

"Never been married, Arthur, so I'm hardly qualified to comment on what 'happily married' actually means. Wife is a pillar of society from what I do know. Maybe he is just bored with her and seeks his entertainment away from home. It must get to you, doing the kind of work our Henry does."

"Yes, I can only imagine. Sick bastards. I've known many a bent copper in my day, helped nail a couple in Scotland once. But I've never come across one into kiddie porn. Sick, sick bastards."

Harvey had long since been happily married. Divorced almost eight years, he kept in regular touch with his two children even though both had surprisingly returned to Scotland to study and work.

The editor of the Evening Gazette had never remarried, preferring to spend his few free hours away from newspaper duties to augment his jazz collection.

"Right, so if we want to beat the so-called big boys we have to run with this story now. That what you're telling me?"

Brits & Bobs: Bob Dylan In The British Isles
by STEVE BUTTERWORTH

Rated five out of five stars by the No. 1 Dylan magazine *Isis.*

Rock 'Til You Drop
by STEVE BUTTERWORTH

Rock 'Til You Drop
(Music stars who never hit 40)

*MURDER...SUICIDE...DRUGS...
ACCIDENTS...NATURAL CAUSES*

THE bad, the mad and the sad deaths of the giants and also-rans of rock. The music world is littered with early deaths, stars taken before their time. Some died tragically, others by their own hand.

Unlike many books, author **STEVE BUTTERWORTH** concentrates on the end of their short lives rather than on the careers of musicians who died before reaching their 40th birthday.

From Johnny Ace – for whom a game of Russian Roulette went badly wrong on Christmas Day – to Mia Zapata – whose killer was brought to justice in 2004, 11 years after her brutal murder.

Contains 13 pages of appendices featuring deaths by cause, date and age.

Rock 'Til You Drop

Sample index

DRUGS

BY DATE